And the Lord went before them by day in a pillar of cloud,

to lead them the way; and by night in a pillar of fire, to give

them light; that they might go by day and by night . . .

BY SOMA MORGENSTERN

TRANSLATED FROM THE GERMAN

BY LUDWIG LEWISOHN

PUBLISHED BY

THE JEWISH PUBLICATION

SOCIETY OF AMERICA

PHILADELPHIA

MCMLV–5715

THE THIRD PILLAR

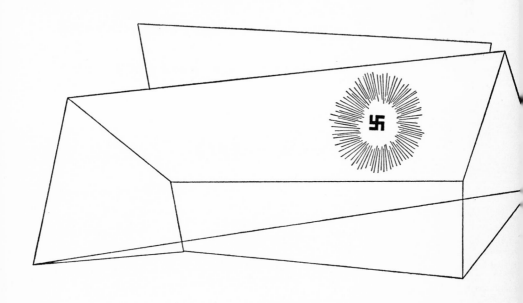

GLOSSARY

Ab Beth-Din : head of the court
Almemor : dais in a synagogue
Athhalta di-Geulah : beginning of redemption
Bar Mitzvah : religious majority
Beth Din : court of law
Hasid (pl. *hasidim*) : pietist
Hatzot : midnight prayer for the rebuilding of Jerusalem
Hillul Hashem : profanation of the Name of God
Huppah : bridal canopy
Ilui (pl. *iluim*) : gifted student
Kaddish : memorial prayer
Kohen (pl. *Kohanim*) : member of priestly family
Kol Nidrei : the opening chant on the Day of Atonement
Malakh : angel
Meshumad : apostate
Minyan : a congregation of at least ten men
Mishpoche : family
Neilah : closing prayer on the Day of Atonement
Rahamin : mercy
Shekhinah : God's presence
Sitra Ahra : the "Other Side," i.e., the devil
Zaddik : righteous, pious man

THE FIRST CHAPTER

It came to pass in that part of the world in which no religion worthy of that name has ever arisen; in which, in truth, all religions save one had died of their own corruption. It came to pass in that part of the world which takes its name from a woman who, according to the legend, pleased its highest god in the form of a cow. It came to pass in Europe.

It came to pass in that time which had grown defiled by the moral defilement of the people known as German. First this people raged in the West of the continent, but soon equipped great armored armies of murderous incendiaries and in swift, predatory marches subdued the entire continent with war and death and fire.

It came to pass in the third month of the fifth year of the war, when a powerful nation from the east, rallying under a red star, had smitten the blood-drunk army of the Germans with fist of steel upon its iron forehead and was driving the reeling monster with mighty tread across the waste, seared lands back to the blood-soaked country of its origin.

It was in a small half-burned border town by the River Seret, which had been liberated from the German oppressors on this very day, that now three Christian publicans found, amid the rubbish which the incendiaries had

1

discarded in their flight, a simple box of white wood which had gleamed brightly amid the dust and rubble of the burned railroad station of the town.

The box was five feet long, two feet in breadth, one and a half feet in height; upon its two narrow sides its clean wood bore an inscription—three lines in square letters, black and heavily marked—which would have been easy to read and interpret, had the publicans known the language in which the inscription was written.

The publicans were in search of food. Like all the human beings and the very animals of the land, they had long suffered from starvation. Because into this land too the murderous incendiaries had crashed in order to rob peasant and worker of bread, the merchant of his wares, the student of his book and the Jew of his life. In true German fashion they had done these things thoroughly during the long, long war and need was sore even in this frontier town.

Since they were hungry, the three publicans suspected some edible thing in the box. Hence they marched into the ruins and possessed themselves of it and carefully carried it across the rubble. They set it down upon the still snow-flecked grass in front of the railroad station in order to open it and to investigate its contents.

But although these three men, by reason of their calling, were well practiced in the opening and closing of all kinds of receptacles and although they had the needed tools in the tops of their tall boots, they applied themselves for a long time, first calmly, then with hasty zeal, finally in their annoyance changing tools and devices, without the slightest success in so much as loosening a single board.

"We can't go on with this thing forever," said the oldest of the publicans. "The roar of the heavy artillery is becoming weaker; we can already hear the rattle of small arms; soon the Reds will march in and, being victors, will share their booty with no one. Let us take the box to a place of safety. A delightful odor comes from it; it must contain something very good. Lend a hand and we will carry the box to my house."

"In my tool room I have a crowbar which is very apt for opening such boxes," said the youngest of the publicans. "Let us hasten to carry the box to my house."

"Above all we must make haste," said the oldest publican. "Let us carry the box to my house. It is true that it is very firmly and tightly nailed down, but surely three publicans cannot fail to open it."

Suspicious of each other after the manner of publicans, the three men contended calmly but stubbornly for a while concerning into whose house their find was to be brought, until in fear of the invading troops which were approaching and here and there becoming visible, they carried the box to the house of the youngest among them, since this house was indisputably the nearest at hand.

The youngest of the three publicans, encouraged by this decision and eager for his own advantage, quickly fetched a wheelbarrow and bent over the box in order to lift it upon the barrow. On the instant he jerked back, as though the box had smitten him upon the chest, and cried out in anger: "You said that an agreeable odor comes from this box? I find it abominable. Who knows what is in it!"

The other two publicans regarded him with astonishment; they exchanged suspicious glances; thereafter they bent down over the box and sniffed at it after a manner common to dogs and publicans. They raised their faces, refreshed and rejuvenated by the fragrance they had inhaled, toward the heavens, as though they were calling upon a higher witness against the incomprehensible folly of their insensitive comrade. Finally with skilled and careful hands they lifted the box and bedded it, with the tenderness due to something precious, upon the framework of the barrow.

"When I was but a lad," said the eldest of the publicans, "scarcely out of school, I worked for quite a while in the pharmacy of a Jew named Monies. The apothecary was a good man and a well-tempered one. He took his calling seriously and was a tireless worker. But he derived a good deal of amusement from his customers, especially from the peasants who came from their villages to the weekly market. Our peasants, as we know, do not like the fragrances of the pharmacy. 'A peasant is better pleased with the stench of his manure heap,' the old apothecary used to say, 'than with some exquisite perfume'; at this he wrinkled his nose. 'Let this be a lesson to us: if a smell meets a nose and the smell seems a stench, it is sometimes the fault of the nose.' This is what the old apothecary used to say. You, Brother, have been a publican here for three years, but your nose is still a real peasant's nose."

"That's Jewish smartness," said the youngest publican in his annoyance. "It's done our Jews a lot of good, their Jewish smartness! Where is he, your clever apothecary? In a crematorium. They say that the Germans make soap of Jewish children and mattresses out of the beards of their elders. The old apothecary was a skinny man; he didn't have much fat for soap. But he did have a handsome red beard. Maybe he is part of a comfortable mattress now, that clever Jew of yours."

"The misfortune of the Jews argues nothing against their wisdom," said the oldest of the publicans. "And what has the apothecary's sad fate to do with his wisdom? Our Savior was a Jew too, and the Romans crucified him. Had the Romans been like the Germans, maybe they would have made soap of our Savior too and—"

"You ought to be ashamed of yourself to talk that way of our Savior," screamed the youngest of the publicans. "You talk like a Red. No wonder. You stuck to the Reds when they ruled us here. You ought to be ashamed of blaspheming so!"

"And you, young man, with whom were you in league? With the German murderers! You'd better be careful, as careful as you can be! The Reds are coming back. They may ask you what became of the apothecary. Maybe they'll ask all of us Christians here what became of the Jews."

4

Meanwhile the audible firing of light field artillery resounded over the burning town again and the dull tumult of an explosion shook the smoking ruins. From among the crumbling walls of a crippled, old alley burst forth filthy and disheveled soldiers in the stamping trot of the heavily armed, yelling, shooting, throwing flames.

"We'd better hide our box in the old synagogue," said the oldest of the publicans. "There are still Germans in town. If they find us with this German box, heaven help us."

"It could be the Reds," said the youngest, while the other two seized the box and hurried in the direction of the synagogue. "Probably it is your Reds," he repeated, grabbing the handles of the wheelbarrow and hastening after the others. "If the Reds find us with this German box, not even heaven can help us."

"They were those Germans of yours," the oldest publican replied. "I see it by the way they trot. Victors don't trot that way. It is the trot of the beaten. Let's stay in the old synagogue until those pestilent creatures have either been driven across the river or been drowned in it."

"For all I care we can wait in the synagogue. You never know. The Germans may come back. Three times within two weeks the Reds were here; three times they were driven out again. So let's await the event of this battle in the synagogue. Then we'll put the box on the barrow and take it to my house; there we will see what is in it that smells so agreeably to you and so ill to me."

The old synagogue stood in the Jewish quarter on a corner from which two alleys started out on their crooked course. It was a broad, flat cube, built of rough stone, weathered to such a blackness as though it had been hewn from a single dark boulder. This somber structure occupied the entire corner space. Although three of its walls, the east wall, the north wall and the south wall, were free and unobstructed, there was no entrance in any of them.

The entrance was in the western wall of the cube. To find it, one had to enter through the gate of a strong iron fence and traverse a small front yard on which the snow was still lying between heaps of clay and withered bushes. This small front yard looked like the gap left by a broken tooth in that row of houses which began with the old synagogue and extended onward toward the west in a narrow row of poor Jewish homes which had been reduced to rubble.

The old synagogue had been so built as to conceal its real height. The foundations had been laid so deep, so very deep into the earth that the great Hall of Prayer was twice as high as would have been assumed from an outside view. A flight of thirteen steps led from the vestibule into the Hall of Prayer below.

In the middle of this Hall stood the Almemor to-

6

gether with the lectern on an elevation of masonry which corresponded in height to that of the entrance. High up on the north wall were the galleries for the women, separated by walls five to six feet in height with a few round glassed spy windows.

The old synagogue was no older than two hundred and sixty years. It had been built upon the ruins of a far older synagogue, which had been destroyed in the days of the uprising of the Ukrainian chieftain Bogdan Chmelnitzky by his Haidamaks. It was probably for this reason that the old synagogue had been sunk so deep into the earth. It was to hide from the enemy. For two hundred and sixty years this had been accomplished. Then came these other murderers to the River Seret and found the old synagogue and its Jews in the city by the river.

These murderers had for two years wreaked their fury upon this town, as upon many others in the Eastern region. Now the town was a ruin, the houses of the Jews were a heap of rubble and the Jews themselves reduced to ashes. Nothing stood except the old synagogue, black and solitary in its corner. For two hundred and sixty years it had stood here as the sign of a blessing; it still stood here, but now as the sign of a curse.

Its outside seemed almost unhurt; the interior was dead. All that was movable had been stolen; all that was tearable had been torn; all things fragile had been broken; all that was pliant had been bent; all that was combustible had been burnt; all that was clean had been defiled; all that was holy had been desecrated.

In the middle of the eastern wall was the very heart of the old synagogue: the Ark with its Torah scrolls. It had been ripped out and burned together with the many scrolls, even as the hearts of those who had devoutly read the scrolls had been ripped out and burned. The air in that great Hall of Prayer was stagnant with the rigidity of a thousand prayers which had been murdered, of a thousand songs which had been throttled, of a thousand sighs which had been quenched.

7

In every corner of the Hall traces of the murderous hands were visible and palpable, of hands that had slain and desecrated, of hands as blasphemous as they were obscene. In the middle of the northern wall where the women's section was, such a hand, an accursed and skillful one, had painted two pictures: the larger one represented the figure of the crucified in the guise of a Polish Jew in caftan, with earlocks, the velvet Sabbath cap with its thirteen marten tails on a blood-stained wounded head. The figure had been drawn with red chalk and its visible heart was in the form of the Red Star of the Soviets.

The smaller picture, to the left of the crucified one, represented a Jewish boy of about thirteen. The thin still-childlike body was also draped in a caftan; the earlocks were curled and of uncommon length; the velvet Sabbath cap with the thirteen marten tails was pushed down deep and crookedly over the delicate face. This younger figure, too, had the gesture of the crucified. But it had not been nailed to the cross. It had been quite obviously placed in its position by bullets through the forehead, through the hands and through the folded feet. This figure had been drawn with blue chalk and again showed a red Soviet Star as its heart.

The images of the two crucified ones were surrounded by a wreath of group pictures, representing men and women in an unbridled, pagan dance. The women were obviously of Jewish blood; they were naked; their gestures were obscene and lustful. The men were in military garb, obviously Germanic; their grimaces jeered and in their hands were whips and firearms. Above the many colored paintings could be read in heavy Gothic letters: The Bloody Wedding Beside The Seret. Below in letters of alternate red and black stood the name of the artist as well as his number in the S.S. group which he had served with heart and hand.

The iron-hinged entry door to the place of worship had been defiled and broken; the four arched windows had been smashed. In this hall, commonly well lit, it was now bright as day and the insolent colors of the murals leaped into the sight of any who stood even on the first step.

Here on the first step of the stair the two publicans placed the box. They looked around. The youngest had left his wheelbarrow in the vestibule. Now he too entered. He sat down on the third step and opened first his eyes and then his mouth and said in a loud voice: "That's thorough work."

"Thorough German work," said the oldest of the publicans. "If these criminals escape unpunished, I shall no longer recognize my God." "It seems to me that they have escaped unpunished," said the youngest of the publicans. "This thing was done two years ago. Even then our bishop said: 'The avenging hand of the Lord has finally reached the unbelieving Jews.' Who is better versed in the ways of Providence, you or a bishop?"

"Our Metropolitan," the oldest of the publicans replied, "took the part of the persecuted Jews. It is said that he keeps hidden sundry rabbis and famous Jewish scholars in his monastery, in order that they may not fall into the hands of the Germans and their confederates. Who is more skillful in interpreting the ways of Providence: your bishop or my Metropolitan?"

"Your pastor, the Metropolitan, put in a good word for the Jews; that is true," said the youngest of the publicans, "but the sheep of his own flock plunged among the Jews like very wolves. If he doesn't know his own flock, that shepherd of yours, how is he to discern the ways of Providence?"

"It is not to be denied," the oldest of the publicans replied, "that your chief pastor knew better. He knew that his flock consisted of wolves and so howled with the wolves. Nevertheless I would not like to be in the skin of your pastor."

"My pastor, your pastor, what sense is there in that talk?" said the third publican who had hitherto been silent. "There were wolves among the Romans and there were

9

wolves among the Greeks. And there were good people in both groups. Alas, alas, that everywhere the good people are too few."

"It is rumored that even among the Jews there were those who sent their own to their death, to save their own skins," said the youngest of the publicans. "It is not for us to sit in judgment on such Jews," said the oldest of the publicans. "Who can say how I or you or you would have acted if such woe had come upon us as came over the Jews? We are responsible only for our co-religionists, for those among our brethren who joined the Germans and raged like wolves among the Jews."

"When the general destruction of the Jews set in," the youngest of the publicans narrated, "I was still living in my village. The peasants said: 'Our Jews are good people; we will do nothing to hurt them.' And the same thing was said by the peasants in Janovka and in Hayvorony and in Denysov concerning their Jews. Thereupon the Germans gathered all the village Jews and drove them into the city. Here they were an indistinguishable multitude. And the peasants of the various villages followed their Jews into the city and here these peasants were an indistinguishable multitude too. And the mob of peasants helped the Germans in the city to destroy the mixed crowd of Jews."

"How many Jews were there in your village?" asked the oldest of the publicans. "There were seven Jewish families among us, that is, forty souls old and young," the youngest of the publicans related. "Of these forty it is said that one young man survived who has been kept hidden by a peasant in a cavern. But no Christian has seen this surviving Jew."

"Assuredly no Christian has seen this Jew, otherwise he would not be alive any longer," said the oldest of the publicans. "Nevertheless since there was one righteous man in your village, your village was better than Sodom. In your village one Christian saved one Jew. Here among

10

us there were six and twenty thousand Jews, among them no less than ten thousand children! How many, do you believe, how many of these six and twenty thousand are still alive here, in this Sodom of ours?"

"It is asserted that a number of Jews are still hidden amid the masonry of the tombs in the old cemetery," said the youngest of the publicans. "It is said that there is a secret subterranean passage which leads from this synagogue to the old cemetery. It is also said that there are among us Christians so devoid of honor that in dark and moonless nights they leave bread which the Jews gather, having come secretly here and then return to their hiding places by way of the subterranean passage. And it is even said that you yourself are one of those who furnish bread to the Jews."

"They are no friends of mine who spread such tales behind my back," said the oldest of the publicans. "What will not people repeat! Is it not also said that uncanny goings-on have been observed in this old synagogue? Do you, for instance, know the story of your pastor, his Reverence Skovronski, who commanded that the blasphemous image of the Savior be scrubbed away from the wall?"

"I heard that tale while I was still in my village," said the youngest of the publicans and laughed. "I knew that Father Skovronski ordered the picture to be removed. And a whole crowd of women came and scrubbed with brushes and with soap and water. And the next day when the priest came to see how well the job had been done, the image was again on the wall as fresh and gleaming in color as when the Germans had first painted it. That was the tale that ran in my village. Do you believe all that?"

"I do not believe it," replied the oldest publican. "But you do not tell the whole story. The priest ordered the picture to be obliterated and it reappeared. You see it there, just as the German Christians painted it. But that is not the whole story."

"You say: German Christians," the youngest inter-

11

rupted him. "How is it possible for any Christian, even though it be a German Christian, to paint such a shameful picture? Among us in my village the opinion ran that the picture had been painted by Jews in order to jeer at our Savior. That is how it must have been."

"That's what your Germans say. What don't they say, now that they're getting frightened," the oldest of the publicans insisted. "The Jews have no paintings in their houses of prayer; every child knows that. Furthermore, look closely: there is not one picture of the Savior; there are two, the big one and the little one. The big one jeers at our Savior and the little one at the Messiah of the Jews. Would the Jews deride their faith in this house?"

"The Jews are capable of anything," said the youngest of the publicans. "It was their intention to deride our Savior. But in order to confuse us concerning the shamefulness of their deed—and that is where the cunning of the Jews comes in—they added the picture of a Jew boy. Every child here knows whom the small picture represents. It is one of the twins of the Torah scribe Zachary. Well, do you suppose that the Jews took this boy to be their Messiah?"

"The face does bear a resemblance to the sons of the Torah scribe; that is correct. The twins were thirteen when they were murdered here together with many other Jewish children. No one knows why the German Christians gave to the smaller picture the features of the children of the Torah scribe. What is well known is the sequel to the story which you began to tell. The priest Skovronski made not one nor yet two, but three attempts to obliterate the paintings. The first time he bade wash away the big one. The second time both. The third time the entire wall was scrubbed clean but after every attempt all that had been seemingly scrubbed away reappeared overnight on the wall."

"It would, of course, be overnight," said the youngest publican. "How could it have happened if not by night? It is by night that the Jews came from their cemetery by way of the secret tunnel and restored the pictures. A man that can write a Torah with a goose quill can paint as well. And he is still alive, that accursed scribe."

"You've lost your good sense, brother," said the oldest of the publicans. "Associating with the Germans has made you stupid. Even if there were some living Jews in the old cemetery and even if there were a secret passage, how could it lead hither from the cemetery, seeing that between the cemetery and the synagogue our River Seret flows in all its breadth and depth? And even though the secret passage had been dug under the bed of the river, how could the Jews paint here by night unobserved? Did not both of the priests, the Roman as well as the Greek, give orders that we should keep an eye on the synagogue and give notice of anything that takes place here?"

"That is because the two priests are contending with each other concerning this synagogue," the youngest publican cried zealously. "They want to make a church of the synagogue, the parson Skovronski a Roman church and the Pope Harasymovicz a Greek church. It is for this reason that they watch over it so eagerly. They have finally agreed not to contend concerning the matter until the war is over. But by that time the Germans will find out what is going on and one fine day blow up the whole building together with the pictures. The Jews are dead. And dead men, even if they were Jews, do not pray. So what is the sense of a synagogue here?"

At that moment a great howling broke out beyond the synagogue. It sounded as though the very hills howled about the city. "Those are the Germans. Thus they cry when they are triumphant," the youngest publican yelled happily as though he wanted to join that victorious howling. "Once more the Germans have the upper hand. I told you it would come about so!"

"Your ears hear what your heart desires to hear, and they hear wrong," said the oldest of the publicans. "It is not thus that the Germans cry their cry of victory. The Germans cry: 'Hurrá! Hurrá! Hurrá!' But this crying—do you

13

not hear it?—sounds: 'Uúrrrah—Uúrrrah—Uúrrrah!' It sounds as though the earth were crying. When the Germans cry, it seems the very voice of hell. Therefore a man is bound to fear them most. Let us go now. The devil is withdrawing toward the West. He is on his way home."

THE THIRD CHAPTER

The three men arose slowly, one after the other, as though each was sorry to have interrupted their conversation prematurely. While the youngest one and the silent one among the publicans turned toward the box and were about to bend over it, they observed with astonished eyes how the oldest as by a sudden determination descended the stairs. With heavy, stamping tread he walked slowly along the whole length of the great Hall of Prayer and remained standing in the corner between the windowless east wall and the great windows of the south wall.

Wide-eyed they watched as the oldest crouched down in that corner, how with seeking hands he groped along the floor and finally lifted up a paving stone with both hands. And now they heard very clearly how with a loud voice—as though he were shouting down a deep well—he cried out: "Michael, it is I, I: Andrej! The Germans have been put to flight. The city is liberated! The air is clean! You can come out safely, Mechzio. Hey, Mechzio, it is I, Andrej!"

"And so it is true after all. There is still a living Jew in our town," the youngest of the publicans said in a mournful voice. "And we had all hoped and believed that the town had been cleared of Jews. And yet here he kept a Jew hidden and gave him the bread, the precious, scanty

15

bread which for years did not suffice to keep our Christians from hunger. That shows you how one of us lied year in and year out, lied and swore falsely. Just a little while ago he denied everything. He is a cunning one. Who would have thought it!"

"I denied nothing; I swore to nothing; nor did I hedge," the oldest of the publicans answered from the place where he stood. "It is you that said I was hiding Jews and giving them bread. I said, whoever speaks so is no friend of mine. Is it not true? Had the Germans heard you speak thus, I would long have been as dead as a Jew. So were you my friend when you spoke thus? No! But you did not betray me to the Germans. Not me. Therefore I will forgive your dangerous talk. But now you can tell it to everyone. Now he who speaks of me as you have spoken of me, is my friend. Now you two can take the box and share its content, whatever it may be, between you. I will take my living Jews and bring them to the Reds and perhaps they will give me bread. So I will get bread for bread, not bread for blood as you got it from the Germans."

"Jews, he said! Did you hear him? So he saved not one Jew but several. Oh, it's enough to make one weep!" The youngest of the publicans was evidently near weeping. But the silent one reminded him with emphatic glances and gestures of the box and so the other gave over lamenting. As a matter of course these two vigorous men prepared themselves to lift between them a not too heavy burden and each put his hands on one side of the box. But both men lost their equilibrium and would actually have toppled over like unskilled people who expect small resistance from a light object which suddenly turns out to be a heavy one.

The two men were ashamed of what they supposed to be their lack of skill. They made their arms tense and uttered a common sound of understanding. Nevertheless they found it impossible either to lift the box or to shift its position by the breadth of a hair. "This box has become as heavy as the whole world," said the silent one. And fear-

16

fully he peered toward the exit as though danger threatened him. "The devil only knows what's in this stinking box," cried the youngest of the publicans. He struck the box with the palm of his hand and with his clenched fist and finally, in his blind rage, he drew back his right leg in order to kick the box. But whether it was that he had drawn back his leg too far, or whether it was that the convulsion of his rage had affected his members—he plunged forward, fell down two steps deeper and for a while lay where he had fallen, speechless and with contorted features.

The oldest of the publicans now walked back slowly the whole length of the Hall of Prayer. Hesitantly he remounted the steps, constantly turning around to gaze at the opening in that far corner which he had not covered again with the stone, although the man Michael to whom he had called evermore insistently had not yet been either seen or heard.

"That this box which we carried here so easily has now become so heavy," the oldest said, "proves very clearly that something is hidden in it which is worth keeping. However that may be, since the two of us carried it here, it is for us to take it to a place of safety. Lend a hand, brother Havryluk!"

Instead of lending a hand, the silent publican drew away from the box and without taking his eyes from it, he said: "I would give a lot to have someone tell me with assurance, whether it was we who brought this little box here or whether it was not perhaps this little box that brought us hither. I wouldn't touch it again even with a finger, this little box which can make itself light or heavy, according to its pleasure. That is nothing for an ordinary publican. I will take good care never to come near it again."

"Nor I," the youngest of the publicans, who had pulled himself up on his legs again, agreed. "I will take good care not to touch this box again. I am running at once to his Reverence Skovronski and tell him what is happening here. The tales that are told are true. Everything here

17

is uncanny. It is certainly the Jews who are guilty of this unnatural mischief. It is our punishment for any one who hid Jews and fed them with Christian bread."

After the youngest of the publicans had run out through the vestibule and had vanished, the oldest said in half tones, as though he were talking to himself: "He runs so swiftly because he has so many horrible crimes on his conscience and has been living for years in constant fear of punishment and retaliation. Now he runs to his confessor in order to report the finding of the box but also in order to notify him that I am hiding Jews here. Thus I think it advisable to inform our Pope concerning the box too. It is a German box. The Germans are adept at all kinds of devilishness. But I am not afraid of a box which is so fragrant. First, too, I must put the paving stone back in its place. It is not a good sign that my Mechzio neither shows up nor answers. In the end my poor friends may still have fallen into the hands of the Germans."

"I cannot deny that I am afraid of this box," said the silent one among the publicans, "and so, if you wish, I will go to my Pope and give him a full accounting. But I do think it all wrong to leave you here alone. I believe you that you have no fear. You have no fear of what has taken place. Well and good. But who can say what may yet happen here?" "I haven't the slightest fear of anything that may still happen here," the oldest publican answered, "Run to the Pope and, in God's name, bring him here at once."

Thus encouraged the silent publican prepared to go. But at the open gate he turned slowly and ruminated a little and asked the other: "Can you remember precisely to which one of us three it occurred to carry the box into the old synagogue: was it I, or you, or was it he, the villager?"

"It was I," said the oldest; "I can tell you that with a good conscience. I remember that very well, because I had another reason when I proposed to bring it here: I wanted to bring the good news to my friend Mechzio as quickly as possible. For a whole week I have been able to

18

leave no bread for him. During the last days of the fight there were too many Germans in the town. It was too dangerous for me as well as for him and for those whom he is protecting."

"If it was you to whom it occurred to bring this strange box here and if you had in addition so sensible a motive, nothing evil will happen to you here. The Germans are gone. Gone and done for! The world is a world again. Torture and death are no longer the reward of a good deed. I'm going to the Pope and bring him with me at once, otherwise the Romans with their Latin will steal a march on us."

Now that he was alone the oldest of the publicans looked about him as though he wanted to make very sure that he was indeed alone. Then he kneeled down beside the box and crossed himself according to the Greek rite, thrice from right to left. Then he set about touching the box with careful, searching hands and made sundry attempts to lift it, turn it, change its position. Since all these efforts were in vain, he stood up in obvious confusion and his heart seemed to have split into two halves: one half, filled with terror, bade him to save himself swiftly from this place— and he did take one or two steps toward the door; the other half, which was full of faith, persuaded him to remain firm—and he stood still.

This inner struggle made him so weak that for a while he leaned his back against the stone wall, powerless to stir a limb. But fate would have it that his faith overcame his fear; and when he was able to breathe freely again and to recover his courage, he at once went down the steps again and tramped on his heavy boots through the Hall of Prayer back to that corner where the gray paving stone lay beside the black square of the opening in the flooring.

This time he lay down flat on the flooring. Supporting his head with his hands he cried down into the depth again with a loud voice: "Mechzio, it is I, Andrej! The Germans have fled and the city is free! Come out, all of

19

you!" And although no voice came to answer him, he did not cease crying out his good news into the depth. Repeating the same words again and again, seeking to render his voice stronger and stronger, he stopped to listen between cry and cry and listened again and again for an answering call.

So absorbed was he in his occupation that he did not hear a troop of soldiers entering the old synagogue. There were six of them, led by an officer. They had trod carefully, seeking to be quiet. At the side of the officer walked the youngest of the publicans; they were already on the first step beside the box, when the oldest of the publicans in sudden fright raised his head and saw the intruders.

"There he is, the old Kalmuck." he heard the officer cry out in the high sharp voice of the Northern oppressors. He recognized the tone and saw at once that these were German soldiers of the frightful storm trooper type.

"You can see, sir, that I told the truth," the youngest of the publicans said eagerly to the officer of the storm troopers. "There where he stands is the opening to the subterranean passage through which the Jews come in secret from the old cemetery and fetch themselves bread. The secret passage leads under the bed of the river to the cemetery. It is all as I reported it to you dutifully and truthfully."

The officer of the storm troopers gave swift and angry orders: three soldiers were to guard the entrance; two were to find out what was the nature of that subterranean passage and report the result on the instant; the sixth, who had a blood-soaked bandage about his head and forehead, he kept beside him.

"Tell them, sir, command them, sir, to destroy the Jews down there at once," the youngest publican said zealously to the officer, while the scouts of the latter hastened down the steps. "His Lordship, your commanding general, who is at the head of this town, has promised us to cleanse the town of Jews. And, by God, he kept his word. Is it his fault that there is a traitor among us who hid Jews and fed them?"

"Don't come! Run! Hide! The murderers are here again!" the oldest of the publicans yelled in frenzy through the opening into the subterranean passage. He was still yelling thus with all his might when the two German soldiers grabbed him with their powerful arms and lifted him high and threw him aside, as though he were some lifeless object, in order to gain the opening of the passage into which they lowered themselves down, each holding the other's hands after the manner of trapeze performers.

"You heard, sir, did you not, how he warned the Jews?" the youngest of the publicans lamented, adjuring the officer again and again not to spare the Jews. The officer now gave the oldest publican, who had picked himself up again, a signal to approach. And since in his fright he did not understand the signal at once, the officer yelled: "Come here, Kalmuck, or I'll finish you off in short order!" And he threatened him with his outstretched revolver.

"How far does the passage lead?" he asked the oldest publican who now approached, pale of face, confused of glance, and stood before the stone stairs. "How far the passage leads I do not myself know. I have never been down there. But it seems to lead to the old cemetery at least."

"Seems! To whom? And why?" the officer asked and sharpened his voice on his teeth, as one sharpens a knife against a whetstone. "Tell me no riddles or I'll finish you off, filthy Kalmuck." "It is exactly and truthfully as I reported to you," the youngest publican said. "You see, sir, he himself admits that the passage leads to the old cemetery."

The officer waved him aside as one waves aside an insect, and did not take his eyes from the oldest publican who said: "Near the old cemetery is the house of a peasant where dwells a brother of this traitor. And this peasant, although the brother of this dog, is a good man. He has helped me to keep those Jews alive. For a time he fed them, for a time I did. Therefore it seems to be true that the passage leads to the old cemetery. But of my own knowledge I do not know it."

"How many Jews are in that subterranean passage?" asked the officer of the storm troopers. "There are eight or nine of them, perhaps ten," the oldest of the publicans answered. He counted them off on the fingers of his hands: "There is old Rabbi Mendele and his brother-in-law Pinchas and the latter's two sons. That makes four. Then there is old Aptovitzer, who was a judge among the Jews, and his son Josko. That makes six. Then there is the Torah scribe, Zacharia, and his wife, Sheva, and their boy, as well as one of the baker's twin daughters. That makes ten. They are all starved and sick and frail and helpless. Your two soldiers have nothing to fear from these, but—"

"Answer what you are asked," the officer interrupted him in his strident voice. "So there are ten of them altogether. Are these Jews all in that subterranean passage?"

Pointing with his finger at the youngest of the publicans, the oldest said: "He said: passage, and you, sir, are repeating that word after him. But is it really a passage? It is a row of clay caverns. Here and there one has to get down on all fours in order to slip from one cavern to the next. Whether they stay constantly in these caverns, I do not know. Sometimes they hide among the graves of the old cemetery. And I must tell you that really there are eleven, rather than ten. There is one among them who is their true protector, rather than I. His name is Michael, but he is known as Mechzio. He is not one of our town Jews. Heaven only knows where he comes from. Perhaps he is from among the Partisans. He is neither ill nor weak nor defenceless—"

"Do you mean to say that he bears arms, this forest fighter?" asked the officer. "Whether he has arms in your sense, sir, I do not know. But he is not defenceless. He is the only Jew who dares to leave the caverns under the earth. Often he wanders about for days on the surface. If he is down there now, among those whom he guards, I am not so sure that your two soldiers will show up again. I just wanted to warn you."

"Warning seems to be your vocation, Kalmuck," the officer roared at him. "First, as I myself heard, you warned your Jews. Now you presume to warn me!" "A jay

23

is but a bird, sir," said the publican, "and yet he warns the whole forest with his shrill cry, whenever danger threatens. Why should not a man warn others?"

After the angry manner of the German commanders, the officer now summoned one of the three soldiers from the vestibule and ordered him to follow the two emissaries down the subterranean passage. "If you will lift three more of the stones," the oldest of the publicans said to the soldier, "you can comfortably descend ten steps and warn your comrades of the violence they will meet. For if Mechzio—" "You are warning again, accursed owl," the officer shrieked in his rage and swung his revolver, with which his hand had been toying throughout.

Meanwhile sharp cries came from the soldiers left in the vestibule and yet other and more distant but also more tranquil answering cries, and after a brief colloquy there came into the Hall of Prayer with rapid step and flushed red face a corpulent priest, accompanied by the taciturn publican, who prudently kept himself behind the priest and in a scarcely audible tone kept whispering in the latter's ear: "There it is, there it still is, that box."

But the presence of the soldiers confused the fat priest to such a degree that, paying no attention to the box, he threw his arms in the air and addressed the officer in tearful irritation: "What brought you here, wretched creatures? The battle is decided. The city is in the hands of the Reds. They have long crossed the river and you are lost."

"We have been cut off, your Reverence, and we know it. But this man here told us about a subterranean passage which is said to lead from this damned synagogue under the river bed to the cemetery," the officer answered with complete self control. "We are a scattered remnant; that is true. But whether we are doomed remains to be seen. A soldier is not doomed, so long as he has a weapon."

"The passage, if one may call it so, may extend to the cemetery, but it does not lead under the river bed. The cemetery is on a hill and the river makes a bend around that hill. And the Reds were beyond that point, on the other bank, early this morning. I am a servant of God and no judge in matters of warfare, but according to all the evidence, the battle on the River Seret has been decided. Lay down your arms and save your lives."

"Life, your Reverence, is not to be despised, but it is not the highest good of a German man. Because it is not, we have conquered Europe. Europe today, the world tomorrow. And I must tell you that, though we are in this place by an accident, being here, we have a duty to perform. Storm troopers are ordered, even when retreating, to blow up all synagogues. Why this one is still here I do not understand. Now my group has no explosives, but I still have thirty men and five machine guns, as you may have observed. That is not much, but it may suffice to force the Reds to use heavy guns against this building and level it with the earth. If any of us survive, such a one may then yield himself up as a prisoner. For this reason I must demand of you, your Reverence, that for your own safety you leave this place at once."

After these words the officer went through the door to the square in front of the synagogue, where he sharply and, as it were, angrily gave his men the commands and instructions concerning the combat around the old synagogue which was about to take place. But when he returned and found the fat priest bent over the box he yelled at him: "You are still here? Away with you! What are you sniffing at here?" The priest raised his tonsured head high and said: "You should know that I came here today not on your account, nor on account of your troops. What brought me here is this box. Regard it well; it bears an inscription in your language. And though I have always understood that language well enough—the inscription on this box does not seem comprehensible."

The officer, becoming aware of the box only now, approached the fat priest and was about to bend down in order to read the inscription, when a second priest entered tranquilly, followed by the youngest of the publicans who had disappeared unobtrusively in order to fetch his pastor. "Now we have two of them," said the officer to the soldier with the bloody bandage about his head. "Our spiritual welfare is certainly well taken care of. I am very sure that this man of God has not come here on your account or on mine either. It is the box that has brought him too, and he, too, is supposed to read and interpret the inscription."

After these words the officer turned again toward the box. Without any attempt to bend down or to read, he announced, keeping his military posture: "This box is German military property. It belongs to the German army. The nature of the contents is a military secret. It is forbidden to sniff around at this box."

THE FIFTH CHAPTER

The two priests regarded each other with a long questioning glance. Then they nodded to each other, as though they were exchanging a silent greeting and thereupon, still eye in eye, they said as with one voice: "Forbidden."

Meanwhile the soldier with the bloody bandage about his head had bent down close to the box and now read almost in a whisper, as though he were reading the inscription to himself alone. Then he raised his wounded forehead to the officer who, with strict military bearing but lowered glance, still stood in front of the box. He said almost as softly as he had been reading: "There is not water enough in the seven seas of the world to wash us clean from the blood and defilement of this gift, Captain of the Storm Troopers, Troop Number 27."

"Who brought this box here? How comes it to be in this place?" the officer began to yell. And he yelled his questions repeatedly, addressing first the wounded soldier and next the two priests and finally the three publicans: "The box is the property of the German army," he yelled, without waiting for an answer. "Whoever touches German army property, no matter how or where, is a plunderer. The penalty for plundering is execution!"

The oldest of the publicans mounted a step nearer to

the officer and said: "We three publicans found this box in a heap of rubble near the railroad station. We thought there might be food in it, and so we brought it here. But easy as it was to carry the box here, so it seems impossibly difficult to move it from this place. You may believe it or not, but it is beyond human power to move the box an inch. Since, moreover, this synagogue has been the scene of strange happenings before, we thought it right to inform the reverend gentlemen of this strange occurrence. There is no question of plundering here."

"Mysterious happenings! Rot! The plundering of German military property seems to me the only uncanny thing that has happened in this accursed hole!" the officer declared. And in his usual strident voice he called out through the gate: "Sergeant-major Hackmueller with four men, report to me here at once!"

At once five storm troopers appeared and the sergeant-major saluted. The officer gave sharp commands: "Carry this box into the open. Kindle a good fire under it, so that nothing remains either of the box or of its contents!" "Will not the smoke betray our presence here?" the sergeant-major asked. "When a whole city is burning, a single pillar of smoke means nothing but one fire among many."

At the beckoning of the sergeant-major the four troopers approached the box, obviously astonished that four men were considered needed to carry a little box a short way. Then they laid their hands upon the box, each of the four laid a hand on one corner of the box. And what had happened to the youngest of the publicans, now happened to the soldiers. They toppled over at the same time; in their fall they slid down two of the steps and found themselves lying across them. Their faces were contorted and their astonishment rendered them speechless. Similarly affected were the witnesses of their fall, the two priests, the officer, the wounded soldier and the sergeant-major.

After a while through the tense silence came the

voice of the youngest of the publicans: "That's what happened to me. Assuredly this thing is caused by the Jews and their black magic. Outside it was a box like any other box. Here it has the magic power to thrust aside four men. So it is true that in this synagogue the devil's magic is at work."

"We have heard from the officer that this box is the property of the German army. You three Christian men brought it hither," said the fat priest, the while he regarded the other cleric with a penetrating and questioning glance. "The Jews, it seems to us, had nothing to do with bringing the box here. And since it is the property of the German army, it is for the officer here to have the box opened and its contents precisely investigated before our eyes."

The other priest, a young tall man with a smooth dark face, agreed with the corpulent priest. "That is the situation. Before we have seen the contents of the box with our own eyes, we shall be in no position to determine whether anything uncanny is going on here. You, publican, will be better advised to be silent and reply only when a question is addressed to you." Both of the clerics nodded at each other again in intimate agreement and simultaneously turned toward the officer of the storm troopers the rejoicing and confident countenances of those who know that it is their vocation to grapple with things beyond the realm of the natural.

The officer of the storm troopers who, to the visible amazement even of the sergeant-major, was but slowly recovering from his dismay at the mishap of the soldiers, and had even now not wholly regained his assurance, yielded willingly to the wish of the priests and gave his consent to the opening of the box. But when the publicans brought forth their tools and were about to begin to work, he waved them irritatedly aside and once more summoned his four troopers who had meanwhile retired toward the gate.

Obsequious to his gestures, the soldiers tore the tools

29

from the hands of the publicans and literally threw themselves upon the box, as though their task were to subdue a dangerous adversary, whom they must show what it means to defy German storm troopers. The sergeant-major, obviously not confident of the result, went swiftly through the gate and returned at once with an arm full of glittering steel tools of reliable German workmanship. He distributed the tools among the soldiers, who got rid of the inadequate implements of the publicans with obvious disgust and now set about outwitting the stubborn box with more effective means. This time the sergeant-major, too, lent a hand with a metal saw and a pair of pincers.

"Sergeant-major," the officer called out to him after a period of effort which already seemed to him too long. "Sergeant-major," he repeated in a voice so mild that it seemed strange both to himself and the sergeant-major, and placed a hand upon his forehead with the gesture of one who seeks to recall a dream. "In what manner did the command reach us to stay in this town and to supervise its destruction? How? When? And whence? And how did it come about that we discovered this accursed Jew-hole?"

Slowly the sergeant-major approached and spoke not like a sergeant-major to his superior officer, but like a man oppressed by care to his fellow in terror: "Sir, you yourself gave these orders; of that I am certain. But now that you ask me I seem dimly to remember that your orders seemed familiar to me even when you uttered them."

"Yes, speaking as man to man, it seems to me too now as though I had dreamed these orders in a dream and had conveyed them to you as one who is dreaming. We were never told to supervise such an action before; I almost fear that no such command was laid upon us. But how did it occur to us to come to this place? Sergeant-major, I am afraid that we have been lured into a trap." The officer pronounced these words in a low voice, almost whispering into the ear of the sergeant-major.

"And who told us about the subterranean passage?" the sergeant-major asked in an equally low voice and in his anxiety addressing the question, as it were, to himself. "That publican yonder, it is now clear to me, was the last one who told us about the passage. But I realize now that he was not the first. It seems to me now as though there were not one nor yet two but that at every crossroads there stood a guide who pointed out to us the way to this synagogue. Was it not so?"

The officer looked about him absent-mindedly, as though he were seeking an answer from those around him. When he perceived that the four soldiers interrupted their work on the box and fearfully raised their eyes to him, he barked at them: "Aren't you done yet?" Instead of an answer the soldiers laid down their tools. Slowly they drew themselves up and one of them declared: "There is nothing we can do. Our tools glide as water glides from oil. The box is so densely made it is as though it were hewn of a single stone."

"It would not be right or proper, if soldiers were able to do a thing at which publicans had failed," the oldest of the publicans asserted with undisguised satisfaction. But he said this neither to the officer, nor to the soldiers, but as his glance signified, to the two priests. The officer, too, now directed his glance to the priests, as though laying the matter from now on before a spiritual court.

Since the priests, however, paid no attention to him, the officer once more turned to his soldiers. "Pack up your tools and get ready for the march," he ordered. "We'll get out of here soon and leave the synagogue and this Jew-box under the guardianship of these clerical gentlemen."

"A while ago, Officer, you declared this box to be the property of the German army," said the fat priest. "And now suddenly you declare it to be a Jewish box! Due to the thoroughness of the so-called cleansing action of your government, there have been no Jews in our city for months and months."

"Jews enough are left in this place. We have just heard it from this Kalmuck here who confessed to us; there are Izzies and Shmuels and even a Torah scribe. He him-

31

self kept them hidden; that fellow over there, your own parishioner, whether with or without the knowledge of his pastor doesn't matter any more. Is it so, publican?"

"It is so, sir. I have kept them hidden here, I, a black sheep, without the knowledge of my shepherd. And that is not a matter of indifference. Yes, there are still a few Jews down there in the passage. According to all human probability they are still alive or were, at least, until your scouts entered the passage. Whether they are alive now is not so certain. But I myself am going to descend into the passage now; if any of them are still alive I will bring them here." With these words the oldest of the publicans leaped down the steps; with the stamping of his great boots he strode through the Hall of Prayer to the dark hole in the far corner and, without asking the permission of the officer or the agreement of the priests, he disappeared into the depths.

"Was it known to you, Chaplain, that a publican kept Jews hidden here?" the older priest asked of the younger. "No," the latter replied, "but the publican belongs to the sheep of your flock. How, then, was I to know?" "My flock, your flock," said the fat priest, "it is all one now. Soon, alas, the Reds will be our shepherds. The black will be white and the white will be black. In the end there will be but a single color. And that will be neither white nor black. Is it not so, Officer?"

"The rule of the Reds will not be of long duration. Let me tell you that at once, gentlemen," said the officer. "As far as your flocks are concerned: I would like to know to whose flock this publican belongs. It was he who told us about the passage and showed us the way to this place. The question is at whose instigation he did this, at yours, Father, or at yours, Chaplain?"

"I did it on my own," the youngest of the publicans declared and moved a little nearer to the chaplain, as though he wanted to place himself and what he still had to say under the priest's protection. "That is to say, I thought I did it on my own. But when just now you raised the question, it seemed to me for a moment as though I had been given an order. But I don't know by whom. It was like a monition."

"Like a monition, eh?" said the officer. "Maybe a monition of your conscience?" And as though he expected an answer not from the publican but from the sergeant-major, the officer turned to the latter and asked him in a low voice: "How long have you been serving with this troop? Was this troop ever in this city? And where was it during Christmas, 1943?"

This quite unmilitary succession of questions convinced the sergeant-major that his superior officer had fallen into his former confusion; he replied as to a man in greater need of consolation than of knowledge. "I have been with troop 27 since its formation and I have treasured both in my memory and in my heart all that has befallen it. Our troop, as you probably recall, was not in this city on Christmas, 1943. We were in Janov. We were in this city once only and that was in the first year of our Eastern campaign, late summer and autumn, 1941. And you, sir, were already with us and had just been appointed our chief."

"Assuredly," said the officer. It did not seem to ease him to have to say this. "Assuredly, I remember quite well. This is not the first time I have been in this town. But how does it happen that this box, which was assigned to our troop on Christmas, 1943, was sent to this place, of all places? And how does it happen that it is we who find this box which evidently was sent astray so long ago? And what have we to do in this uncanny place?"

"You must not call this place an uncanny place. It is the right place," a voice was heard to say at this moment. And to those who heard the voice it seemed as though they had become aware of the words ere yet they had become aware of the stranger who had entered unseen and unperceived and now stood in their midst.

"By what right do you sneak in here among us? What have you to do here?" the officer roared at the stranger. "Sergeant-major, throw this intruder out, and warn your men to admit no one else." The sergeant-major, as though he did not hear the command of the officer, addressed the stranger: "It seems to me that I have heard your voice somewhere and not even long ago. Who are you?"

"I am a Messenger," said the stranger. "I showed the way to you and to your officer. It was I who stood at the crossroads in order to show you the right way." "The aberrant way, you had better say, had you not? Now I do recognize your voice, false guide that you are. You are probably Jewish and you probably believe that your time has now come. You represented yourself to be a harmless guide, while spying for the Reds, and thus you led us into this trap."

"I am, it may well be said, a Messenger. And in a certain sense I may be said to be Jewish. That is not open to doubt. I pointed out the right way to you, Officer, since it is the way which brought you and your fellows to the right place. In whose service I am will become clear by and by to you and the like of you. It will become so clear that your eyes will be dazzled. And you are not to ask me further questions, Officer. Whatever comes or goes, you are guilty beyond all words."

The officer turned to the two clerics: "Tell this Messenger who has the isolence to address me thus, that he is not to rely too greatly on his masters. The Reds will soon be here but ere they come I can blow out his little Jewish light, so that he has no time to gather breath for another insolent word. Who is the man? Do you know him? Is he a native here?"

"Whether he is from here, none can tell. Before your cleansing process there were six and twenty thousand Jews here," said the chaplain, "How should we have known them all? What we can say is this, we have never seen him—" "—and want to know nothing of him," the fat priest added. "We were not the keepers of the Jews here."

"Even as Cain did not wish to have been the keeper of his brother Abel after his crime," said the Messenger. "You dare to say here: before the cleansing process? You mean, before the defilement! Before a murderous defilement so filled with blood that the earth cannot absorb it, that the earth is throttled by this ocean of blood and cries out to heaven—unheard by the murderers, unheard by their confederates, unheard by the witnesses, heard only by the victims and granted a hearing in heaven!"

"He acts in the service of the Reds and uses the language of Scripture; so he must be a Jew," said the chaplain to the fat priest after a period of silence and trembling, during which the former had recovered his speech and the latter his hearing. "So long as the Reds have not arrived, he, being a Jew, is in your power, Officer. You may treat him according to the law of your land. He is no concern of ours. We were summoned here on account of the box. And the box, according to your own declaration, is the property of the German army. Let us then take our leave. We will soon have trouble enough with the Red victors."

"You were summoned hither on account of this box; that is correct," said the Messenger. "And as you were called at the right time, so you will also be dismissed at the right time. As far as the officer here is concerned, he, too, as well as his men, have been commanded to come here on account of the box. And he will remain here until he has been discharged as one upon whom judgment has been passed."

"Who would here have the power to condemn me, or even the right?" the officer yelled. "You have indulged your insolence here far longer than should have been permitted. Sergeant-major, cause this insane Hebrew to be bound and placed against the wall." And in token of his determination to act after the German fashion, the officer raised his pistol toward the Messenger.

"It were best to place me against that painted wall," said the Messenger and pointed with a finger of his left hand toward the wall which bore the images of the two crucified ones. While the officer involuntarily followed this gesture with his eyes, the Messenger tapped his hand as gently as a grown person might jestingly tap the small hand of a child. The pistol dropped from that hand and

36

the Messenger caught it in his own, without taking his eyes from the officer.

"Have you not permitted enough crimes with those hands of yours and even painted paintings," the Messenger added and flung the weapon with unerring hand in a visible semi-circle into the opening that led to the subterranean passage. "Your action is swifter than your speech and your speech swifter than your thought, Officer. I said that you and your men will come under judgment here. And you? You are in haste and speak at once of condemnation. That is not a good thing to do. I am a Messenger. It is not my business to instruct you. But you must understand that arms are not tolerated in the place of judgment. Be guided by the example of your sergeant-major. He, too, was a good German murderer, but as a thoughtful man he will at once gather the arms of all your men and his own and throw them in a heap outside of the synagogue."

To everyone's astonishment the sergeant-major did exactly that. With great deliberation he gathered together the weapons of his fellows, the while the Messenger nodded to him in friendly fashion. But as he was about to lay down the assembled weapons on the stair near the box, the Messenger spoke to him sternly: "Things so impure must not be near what is pure. Carry them out!"

While the sergeant-major with his arms full of weapons went up the stair and out into the open, the Messenger descended the steps; he traversed the entire Hall of Prayer and remained for a space in front of the north wall in ecstatic contemplation of the paintings. But the way in which he descended those steps impressed the priests more deeply than anything, whether word or deed, which they had yet witnessed. The Messenger had his own way of moving. He neither crooked his knees nor did either of his feet tread out beyond the other. Although he had to descend the steps, he seemed to give his body from step to step a light lift, after the manner of a bird who is about to fly. In an instant he had rather glided down the steps than descended them.

37

"This Red partisan has evidently escaped from a circus," said the officer to the returning sergeant-major. "We're being befooled by a juggler who is both a tight rope artist and a hypnotist." "Officer," said the sergeant-major softly: "my men demand the return of their weapons. They are determined to sell their lives dearly." "That is well," whispered the officer. "Go out and stay with the men. I think I am a match for this clown."

The two priests did not take their eyes from the Messenger. They stared toward the painted wall while the Messenger stood in front of it. Nor did they take their eyes from him when, sad of countenance, he turned away from the pictures and in his own strange manner once more momentarily traversed the Hall of Prayer and with bird-like lifts of his body glided up the stair once more.

"Sir," said the fat priest to the Messenger who once more stood near the box, "Sir, you said that we had all been summoned hither on account of this box. Now, as far as that is concerned, it was the publicans who informed us two concerning this matter, because we had given orders that we were to be informed about whatever happened in the synagogue. It was our plan to build a church here. How can it be that we are called hither to submit to a court?"

"Cease from these vain excuses," said the Messenger. "According to you, you are a priest. As such you should know that the hand which summons you here does so in this world by indirection. You have caused this wall to be washed. First it was only one picture that did not please the priests. But when you found that the first could not be washed away, you attempted to obliterate them both. Thereafter you sought to wash clean all the pictures and all the blood soaked hands. Is it not so? Thrice I had to reconstruct the pictures."

"I always did say," the youngest of the publicans spoke to the priests; "I always did say that the Jews painted the pictures over and over again. And so it was. That shows you what they are capable of; and it's due to the fact that Jews were kept hidden here."

"This explains a good deal," the officer agreed. "Since he seems to know everything, perhaps this Messenger will throw some light on this tricky box. How is it that it cannot be moved? Tell the truth, Jew! You tricked me out of my gun by a bit of prestidigitation. But out there I have weapons and warriors enough to deal with you according to my liking." The two priests exchanged a look of mutual understanding. Thereupon the younger of them said to the Messenger: "That question seems to us a very proper one. Tell us, Messenger, what tricks you're playing on us with this box?"

"I perceive that you need unmistakable signs. Mere hints do not suffice you. Well, you shall have them, these signs. First of all, it will be advisable from now on to speak of a shrine or reliquary rather than of a box." "Nonsense! Shrine!" The officer cried in renewed rage toward the Messenger. "This Jewish b— bo—" Suddenly his outcry broke. His tongue was heavy and his lips hung down like an idiot's. In his reddish blue face his eyes protruded like the eyes of one being throttled.

"You behold now that the tricks of this juggler are not simple ones. You will be bereft of speech until you give me a signal that you are ready to call and consider this a shrine as such in all reverence. You are now dumb but not yet deaf. Open therefore your ears and hear: so long as that remains hidden between these boards what has been entrusted to them, so long are these boards a shrine. When the purity which is now in it will have been taken from the shrine, then will these boards which, as you said, are German military property, be once again, as far as I am concerned, what once they were, namely, a box; as far as you are concerned, however, they will be a coffin."

"Let him beware, this mad man, that he does not now vent his rage against himself, as he has vented it against the very endurance of the world. Else these boards will be his own coffin in which he will be carried out, condemned and self-condemned, even before the court has pronounced a sentence over him and over all his kind and over all his confederates, here and everywhere." The Messenger addressed these words directly to the priests who gazed down upon the shrine as though it had only now become worthy of their attention.

"We see the shrine and we read the inscription," the corpulent priest said, "we seem to understand the words of the inscription and no less the words which you are speaking to us. And yet—you must forgive me if I do not know the terms in which you are to be addressed—we do not understand the meaning of the inscription nor scarcely the connection between its words and yours."

"You see what you can; you understand as much as you can. It will suffice to enable you to follow the order of the court. It matters little how you address me." With a sharply crooked finger he pointed to the officer. "You addressed him as: 'Sir,' meaning, as it were, Master. Address me as Servant or Messenger." Thereupon the younger of the priests opened his mouth and asked: "Messenger, what is hidden in that shrine?"

"They do not see because they would not believe their own eyes, Messenger," said the silent one among the publicans, "even as for years they refused to believe what they had seen with their own eyes. I, Messenger, I now have a vision of a figure, young and frail, quite like that one which is delineated on the wall, the smaller one I mean, oh, like a brother to it: the one in the shrine and the one on the wall—they resemble each other like twin children."

"You have the right insight, publican. It will be remembered in your favor. But since you, priest, have asked the direct question, I will answer you according to your understanding: in the shrine there is, according to your Roman way of speaking, when you use the language of ritual consecration, in that shrine is the CORPUS CORPORUM.

41

Does that suffice you?" "You must mean the *corpus delicti*, Messenger," said the younger priest.

"Since you, O priest, did not ask a direct question, but since you speak Greek when you use the language of ritual consecration, to you be it said: in this shrine there is Το Σόμα τῶν Σομάτων. Does that suffice you?" "You must then mean: not only an image?" said the corpulent priest.

"Will we be examined as witnesses, when the court takes up its procedure?" asked the younger priest. "The procedure has already set in. All that you have said here has been heard and received and recorded as evidence." "When did it begin, this procedure?" the corpulent priest asked. "Immediately after the disarming of this mad man." "But that is a procedure beyond all use and order, Messenger," the young priest indignantly interposed. "As far beyond all use as the crimes which will be judged here. And yet not beyond all order. What do you know about the orderly procedure of this court?"

"When did this court begin to sit?" the younger priest asked. "This court is not dependent on the change between day and night. Its session is continuous. So long as these crimes do not cease which have plunged a world into night and darkness, so long will its procedure continue. Perhaps even long thereafter. That will depend upon the sentences of the judges who will sit in this court. Do you not see the judge who is already sitting on the Almemor yonder? You do not see him yet because you do not yet believe in the existence of the court; you still seek a way out. Do you see the judge, publican?"

"I saw him coming. When you, O Messenger, threw away the weapon of the officer, he mounted swiftly from the passage below to the Almemor. But now I scarcely see him," said the taciturn publican. "He is the narrating judge," the Messenger instructed him. "So soon as he will have begun his narrative, he will become visible even to those who choose to be blind. His narration is the first capital part of the proceeding. We have reached the end of the introductory part. The narrating judge can now at any moment begin his narration."

"If we are witnesses, will we not be sworn in?" the younger priest desired to know. "That is not customary in this court," said the Messenger. "This court cannot be deceived, nor is it well for you that you volunteer to be a witness before your eyes are clear enough to see even the narrating judge." "I can see the judge again!" exclaimed the taciturn publican. "The way in which he hides his hands in the sleeves of his caftan reminds me of our Aba Aptovitzer, who used to be a judge in this town." "It is well that at least one of you sees him. Now the narrating judge can begin," said the Messenger, and all conceived of these words as a demand that the judge should begin.

Now the narrating judge raised his voice and spoke. "It came to pass four years before that year in which the defilers of creation, according to their babble, seized power. And it came to pass in the market place of this town. It happened that the Torah scribe Zacharia Hakohen was returning from Morning Prayer in the synagogue. In the middle of the market place he saw a stranger surrounded by a great pack of dogs. From the stranger's shoulders there hung down two sacks, a sack from each shoulder, after the manner of shepherds and beggars. And these sacks were bread sacks of coarse linen. The sacks were full of that kind of white bread which pious women twist and bake in celebration of the Sabbath. The Sabbath loaves in both sacks were sliced and the stranger threw the bread to the dogs, slice by slice.

"The Torah scribe, who lived in great poverty, in whose house bread was not plentiful and was white only on holy days, was greatly astonished that the stranger should cast this good fresh bread, fragrant even from afar, in such quantity to dogs. In his astonishment he approached the stranger, as closely as he could, because of the tumult of the dogs who in their greed formed almost a solid mass about him.

"Although the pangs of hunger attacked him too, for

it was nearly ten o'clock and the Torah scribe, according to his daily habit, had been in the synagogue since early morning, he yet continued to linger and silently to watch the man's strange doings. The longer he lingered, the greater the pack of dogs seemed to become, nor did there seem to be an end to the supply of bread in the sacks, although the stranger did not cease to throw it out with full hands.

"And so the Torah scribe plucked up his courage and made his way through the ravenous pack and greeted the stranger with the greeting of Peace and asked: 'Whence do you obtain all this good bread?' 'And Peace to you, too,' the stranger replied. 'I am a beggar. I go from door to door and pious women give me what has remained over from the Sabbath loaves.' 'Pious women give you this good bread and you cast it before the dogs,' said the Torah scribe in a tone of mild admonition.

" 'I have been wandering from town to town, from market place to market place and I have been doing the same thing, and not a single soul has paid the slightest attention to what I was doing. They are all too busy buying and selling. You are the first who has seen me and asked me. Therefore, you shall be the first among all Jews to whom the meaning of what I do shall be interpreted.' Thereupon the stranger ceased throwing the bread. He turned his clear and tranquil eyes to the scribe and said: 'On a day not too far off murderers and incendiaries, armed to the teeth, will invade this land. They will take the bread from your mouth and the air from your breathing. They will cast your bread before the dogs and the life of a Jew will be cheaper than the life of a dog. Since you have truly seen me, I have given you warning. Now I will wander on from city to city, from market place to market place, and he who truly sees me and asks me, him will I warn, even as you have been warned, Zacharia Hakohen. Go your way and ask no more.'

"The scribe did as he was bidden. In great dismay he left the market place, as fast as his old legs would carry him. On reaching his house, he felt a great weariness over-come him; he sat down on the clay bench in front of his house to recover his breath but also to pull himself to-gether and hide his dismay from his wife who was sickly and fearful.

"Depressed and heavy of heart, although recovering his breath, he was about to rise from the bench when he heard the sound of bright and cheerful laughter. It was the laugh of a woman; it came from the window of his room, and it seemed strange to him although the voice was a familiar one. It was the voice of his wife. And she was laughing. Now the wife of the Torah scribe was a woman constantly grieving, as the years went on, over her barren-ness. He had not heard her laugh for a long, long time, and this cheery sound rejuvenated his heart like an unex-pected favor of fortune.

"In order to enjoy the healing of this happy sound, the scribe remained seated on the bench. And now he heard another voice, the voice of a stranger, speaking clear-ly and unmistakably in his room and saying: 'Well may you laugh, Sheva, wife of Zacharia Hakohen; well may you laugh, even as your arch-mother Sarah laughed, when the messenger announced to her that, though it was late, she would conceive and bear a son.'

"The voice of the stranger did not seem wholly un-familiar to him, and the scribe strained his memory to the utmost to recall whose voice it was which now, once more interrupted by his wife's laughter, continued as follows: 'Your arch-mother Sarah was older than you, Sheva, and she bore one son. You, however, will bear twins, two sons; one of them, O Sheva, wife of Zacharia Hakohen, you will bear as a consolation for your people, the second as a con-solation of the other peoples.

" 'To the first born of the two you will give the name Nehemiah and to the second son the name Jochanan. And you will keep them pure and guard them as the very light of your eyes. And so, too, will your husband. You will make no difference between your sons, neither in your love nor in your instruction of them, even as there will be no difference between their bodily being or their characters.

"'And to Reb Zacharia be it said, that he is to instruct his boys from their tenderest age in the service of the Kohanim. For they are both born to be a blessing, different only in this, that one is destined to console his own people, the other to console the world's peoples when these peoples, to the sorrow of the Creator Himself, will take it into their minds to separate themselves from this people in the days of sorest need.

"'And you are to forget whatever has been announced and proclaimed to you by my voice, O Sheva, wife of Zacharia. Only a monition will remain to you of this annunciation, even as a sweet whiff remains in a vessel which was once filled with fragrant oil. And this will be equally true of Zacharia, the Torah scribe, who now hears me with his own ears, even as he saw me with his own eyes. Peace and blessing be upon you and upon your husband.'

"When the scribe suddenly pulled himself together in the vibrant silence which had set in, he perceived that he had fallen into a light slumber on account of his great weariness. Refreshed by this unaccustomed rest, he arose and entered his house with careful steps. In his work room Sheva was sitting in front of the table, which was half covered with parchment, some on which he had already been writing and some that was yet blank. Her lucid forehead, half covered with a head kerchief, gleamed; her eyes were lowered and fixed upon the empty part of the table where, clean as the parchment and of the same hue, there stood a little open sack half filled with fragrant, sliced white bread.

"Seeing this little sack of bread, a great fright came over the scribe. He uttered a cry and burst into tears. His wife arose swiftly from her seat; nimbly as a young girl she approached her husband and looked at him with a glance from her blushing face, even as she had looked upon him on that first day, upon which they had been permitted to meet as bride and bridegroom on their wedding eve. They took each other's hands, and both wept. She, being a woman, wept for happiness. He, being a Torah scribe, wept for the fear of God.

" 'Today you will break your fast with this good bread,' said the woman, when they had wept their fill. 'There was a beggar here. I gave him a piece of our bread and he, just imagine, took this little bag full of bread and went into your work room and put it on your table.' 'We will keep this bread for the consecration of the Sabbath,' said the scribe. 'But today is only Monday, Zacharia; it will be stale by Sabbath.' 'The bread of this beggar will not become stale; let us count the slices and over each slice pronounce the benediction on a separate Sabbath. It will remain fresh as long as it lasts. You will see that, Sheva.'

"And once more they clasped each other's hands and loosened them, and they counted the slices in the little bag and then put them back into the bag. And they found that the bag contained twice eighteen, that is, six and thirty slices of Sabbath bread.

"And on each of the subsequent six and thirty Sabbath eves the scribe pronounced the blessing over a single slice and broke it and the two of them ate of it. And when it was the turn of the very last slice to be blessed and eaten in consecration of the Sabbath, it was as fresh and fragrant as though it had just been baked and cut.

"And it was on that six and thirtieth Sabbath, that the wife of the Torah scribe was brought to bed and bore two sons, even as that voice had foretold to them in their dream. For the wife of the scribe, too, believed that she had fallen into a doze on that morning and had dreamed her happy dream. About the beggar and the dogs on the market place the scribe had spoken no word to his wife."

"Though the scribe had not spoken of the beggar and his warning to his wife, he had told the tale of the man and the dogs to his friends and neighbors on the very day of its occurrence. That very evening he told the story in the old synagogue both before and after prayers. On his way to the synagogue and also on his way home he lingered daily for a while on the market place and he came to repeat the tale and the beggar's warning, as though it had become an addition to the prescribed prayers.

"People listened to him both in the House of Prayer and in their own houses. One or another who listened became thoughtful or even sad. Rarely did anyone show either fear or consternation. On the market place the scribe met the fate of the beggar: some would not see him, others would not hear him. They were too busy buying and selling. But the scribe was not to be discouraged. Over the weeks and months he did not grow weary telling his tale in the houses and on the market place. But even as telling his story became habitual, so his hearers came to listen merely out of courtesy. Hearing the venerable man, they began to shake their heads over him and to treat him with open pity, as one whose wits had grown feeble in his later years.

"One evening, on the Feast of Purim, when exceeding

merriment reigned even among the Jews in the old synagogue, a man still young approached the Torah scribe and, surrounded by a merry audience, told the company the following little story as part of the Purim fun: One fine day Herschel Ostropoljer, the well known jester, was taking a walk on the market place. There he saw a beggar who had a sackful of bread and threw it piece by piece before the dogs who ran toward him from all the corners of the market place. 'Why do you throw all that good bread to the dogs, scoundrel?' Herschel cried out to the beggar. 'What am I to do with all this bread?' the beggar cried back to him. 'Wherever I knock at a door, a good Jewish woman comes out and gives me a piece of bread. How much bread can a single man eat?' 'Why do you take more than you can eat, scamp?' Herschel cried again. 'When a woman gives you something, you must take it,' the beggar answered and laughed; 'otherwise women will get out of the habit of giving.' 'You're a wise man,' Herschel Ostropoljer said admiringly to the beggar. 'When a woman offers you something, just take it.'

"Now it was clear to the Torah scribe into what his story had been turned in the course of the years, and amid all the extreme merriment of Purim his heart was saddened with the sadness of the world. But all those about him laughed, the bearded pious men and the beardless enlightened men, the old as well as the young. Even the children, with the Purim rattles in their hands, laughed along with the grownups. Only his own children did not laugh. They were not yet quite four years old and they too had rattles in their hands. But the sadness of their father saddened them and they looked upon him with the aware and melancholy eyes of the *Ilui*, the child genius.

"Now the scribe understood how in the course of the years his story had turned him into the town fool. He fell silent in his pain and shame and from that Purim evening on he told the tale no more. Soon, too, it fell into forgetfulness and the scurrilous little anecdote, born of the frivolousness of the Purim evening, took its place as being obviously more pleasing to the people.

"From this time on the days and most nights of the Torah scribe were dedicated to the instruction of his two sons and to his reverent writing of the holy letters. He was on the threshold of old age, and since his late-born boys were only five, he taught them rather with the mild affection of a grandfather than with the stern insistence of a father.

"The two boys, being identical twins and thus scarcely distinguishable one from the other, so, too, they were quite alike in the swift grasp and joy in learning which is found among pious Jewish children. Although somewhat fragile physically, they took no harm from any of the common ills of childhood and their parents were spared any anxiety concerning their well-being.

"Only once did the children incur great danger. As in all towns built beside a river, the youth of our town played during the summer days of vacation for long hours beside the banks of the river. And from early childhood on our boys were eager and expert swimmers. So, too, were the children of the scribe. One day, it was the eighth day of the month of Ab, the river was swollen on account of copious rains and the sons of the scribe, who stayed together even amid the play and turmoil of the children, were caught in a vortex of the river. In imminent danger they clung to each other and sank below the surface.

"The other children, through the noise and excitement of their games, whether in the water or on the bank, were not conscious of the mishap and even the boys' cry for help was not heard. But it happened that the water carrier, Senderl, who was crossing the bridge with his buckets, heard the cry. He got rid of his buckets, leaped from the bridge into the river, and succeeded in dragging the two children who clung close together out of the whirlpool and swimming with them to the shore.

"This water carrier was a man with a great, coarse body, but of a gentle and serene nature. Because he some-

51

what resembled one of the municipal publicans, Havryluk, the jeering jesters of the town called him so. In the course of time everyone used this name. And since he was a very patient man, even the children addressed him as Havryluk.

"On the Sabbath of the week, during which the water carrier had rescued the sons of the Torah scribe, he was called up to pronounce the blessings over the Torah. After the ignorant man had pronounced the additional blessing which is obligatory upon one who has escaped danger of death, hesitantly and not without assistance from the precentor, the venerable Rav of the city arose and approached the water carrier and said to him in a voice so loud that all who were in the synagogue could hear him: "May your strength increase, Reb Senderl." And from that Sabbath on none in the city called him otherwise than Reb Senderl.

"After the accident in the river the scribe and his wife redoubled their vigilance. They dedicated all the hours of their days to the supervision and instruction of the boys. Nevermore did they leave them out of their sight, not when they studied, nor when they played. If the mother left the house in order to seek out a neighbor woman or to make her purchases, the door of the scribe's room was open so that, sitting over his parchments, he might yet hear the voice of the children while they were at play in the house or before it. And the children were permitted to enter their father's workshop if they should need to speak to him.

"These children, moreover, even as from their tenderest years on they possessed a measure of understanding and a zeal for learning, so, too, were they of an early maturity in manners and morals. And so it was almost a year before either of them made use of this permission. Their reverence for their father's pious occupation kept them from interrupting the quiet of his study.

"It was not until they were in their eighth year that one of them, in spite of the circumstances, came loudly weeping into the scribe's study and broke in upon its silence with a moving accusation against his brother. 'We

52

were playing hide and seek and when it was my turn I found a very good hiding place. And I waited for my brother to search for me. And I waited and waited. But when I was convinced that he could not find me and came out of my hiding place, I saw that he had not looked for me at all.' This was the tale the boy told and he laid his face upon the knees of his father and wept bitterly.

" 'I understand your pain,' the Torah scribe said to his son. 'You share this pain of yours with the Creator of the World. He, too, hides Himself. He, too, expects us to seek Him out. And we do not seek Him.' And the Torah scribe wept, too, and mingled his tears with those of his son.

"At that the other son entered the room and declared calmly that he had begun to read in a book, the while his brother was seeking a hiding place, and how he had thus wholly forgotten both the game and his brother. And thus in an instant all this childish woe was allayed.

"Before the brothers, now quite reconciled, left the study, in order to resume their play, one of them said to his father: 'We hide ourselves merely as a game and for amusement. But why does the Creator of the World, blessed be His Name, hide Himself? Were I He, blessed be His Name, I would show myself everywhere and to all men.'

"The other brother said: 'Were I the Creator of the World, blessed be His Name, I would show myself only to Jews, even as He showed Himself to Moses, our teacher, face to face.' Thereupon hand in hand and in complete harmony the brothers returned to their play.

"When he was alone again after this first occurrence of a difference of opinion between his sons, the scribe recalled for the first time that voice in his dream which had foretold the birth of the children. It was hardly vivid enough to be called a memory. Gently as the wing of a dragonfly may stir the moveless air over a tranquil water, so gently did the recollection of his dream and the voice in the dream stir the soul of the Torah scribe, the voice that

53

had left behind the echo of these words: 'Only a monition will remain to you of this annunciation, even as a faint sweetness remains in a vessel which was once filled with fragrant oils.'

"But the more vigorously the scribe searched in his memory, by so much the breath of that memory became farther and more diaphonous. And as he dipped his goose quill into the ink-well and continued his work and determined to question his children once more in the matter of this difference of opinion between them, it seemed as though this first and only conflict between them faded from his consciousness too.

"Next day the father overheard a conversation between his sons who sat on the bench in front of the house and in brotherly harmony conversed in the peculiar intonation of Talmud students. 'When the Messiah comes the chosen people will return to the Holy Land. And there our redemption will set in. *Athhalta di-Geulah*,' said one of them. The other replied: 'When the Messiah comes, the whole world will be a Holy Land. Who shall teach Torah to the world's peoples if not the chosen people?'

"The Torah scribe could not distinguish the voice of one of his sons from the voice of the other. And so he arose and listened and looked out at the window, in order to determine which of his two sons was of the one, which of the other opinion.

"But the children, although they could not see their father at the window, nor had heard him step to the window, did not continue their discourse. Nor did they resume it, although the scribe listened for quite a space of time at the window.

"Persuaded by paternal care or, perhaps, only by curiosity, the scribe went out to his children and sat down beside them. After he had asked first Nehemiah and afterwards Jochanan some questions of minor significance and had received satisfactory replies, he turned the conversation with all possible caution back to the subject of the precedent discussion.

"With the zeal of true Talmudic students, who are always ready to plunge into learned controversy, the boys at once responded to the stimulation of their father. But as the scribe attempted to pin down each boy in respect of his expressed opinion, the discourse became confused. Each agreed with the opinion of the other; the usually swift recollections seemed to fail them; the still childlike and tender skin of their wise little foreheads seemed to be clouded as by pain and the light in the aware eyes of the *Iluim* to be extinguished.

"And since the Torah scribe did not desire in this instance to cease from his insistent questioning and so continued to try to determine once and for all what Nehemiah and what Jochanan had said, he soon seemed to arrive at a point, though he was sitting beside them, at which he could no longer distinguish which of them was Nehemiah and which of them Jochanan.

"The Torah scribe understood that he had touched upon a forbidden matter although he could not remember just what had been forbidden. He had a presage that in a hidden twin sense, which it was not for him to search out, his house had been fated to receive a One which was Two and a Two which was One. And with this presage a secret fear stole into the heart of the scribe, such as can arise only from a deep monition."

"In our town there was yet another set of twins. These were girls, scarcely a year younger than the sons of the scribe. Their father was a baker. His well-known bake house, in which there was room both for the shop and for the dwelling of his family, stood on the market place in that old row of houses, which also included the Talmud school.

"The children of the scribe were aware of the children of the baker, as these were aware of them. But for a long time they did not really know each other. Although he was a poor man, the scribe was a pious and learned son of generations of the pious and learned, while the baker, though well provided with worldly goods, was an ignorant man of business, the son of a baker and the grandson of a teamster. If to this difference you add the difference of sex, it is understandable that the sons of the scribe and the daughters of the baker grew up even in a small town in two different worlds.

"But even though the children of the scribe and the children of the baker did not associate with each other, yet from time to time they saw each other from afar and a few times a year they came in closer contact, especially on the High Holy Days when nearly all the children of the city crowded on the grass plot in front of the old synagogue.

"However, the sons of the scribe were ten years old when, for the first time, they came to know the twin daughters of the baker and spent a whole day in the same room with them. This took place in the week preceding the Paschal Feast in the great bakery in the house of the baker. According to an ancient custom the pious people of the city assembled there annually in order to make their contribution to the baking of the matzoth for the poor and needy. Young and old, poor and rich—they were all there. Whoever had the will to lend a hand, was welcome to share in this benevolent work. The largest baking room of the most important bakery in the town could scarcely hold these voluntary bakers.

"The baking of the matzoth is an equally pious and merry task. All the children of the town wanted to help. The fun in baking matzoth which the children enjoyed came from the great and obvious haste which the adults use. This haste is necessary in the baking of matzoth, in order to eliminate any possibility of the contamination of the unleavened by leaven. Haste in this occupation is, moreover, a pious gesture by which the bakers are reminded of the great and holy haste of our ancestors when they baked in preparation of their hasty departure from Egyptian bondage and their swift entry into freedom.

"Now whenever haste is necessary, work must be largely divided. Hence, from time immemorial we observe in the baking of matzoth a significant as well as useful division of labor. We discriminate between those who pour the dough and those who knead it, those who cut it into cakes and those who smooth it, those who keep the oven hot and those who shove the cakes into the oven, not to speak of the carriers and the expert bakers.

"The finest and the merriest task, so apt to delight the heart of children, is that of using the little cog wheels. In order to prevent the matzoth from rising in the heat of the oven and to keep them flat, one passes from time to time small, handy cog wheels over the smooth squares or

57

circles of dough. This is more play than work, and so a game for children.

"Though it is a game, it must be learned. The sons of the Torah scribe found this out soon enough, the first time they tried to handle the little cog wheels. Scarcely had they taken their place at the proper tables and made their first, awkward attempts, when the two daughters of the baker came up and quizzically surveyed what the boys had done. With the self-importance of little girls they began at once to instruct the embarrassed newcomers. One of the little girls, swift of gesture and arch of glance, said to Jochanan: 'That's not the way to do it!' And she took the little cog wheel out of his hand; with swift fingers she rolled it over the soft surface of the dough and in an instant had completed the pointed lines of a perfect piece of matzoth. The other girl did the same thing for Nehemiah. This second girl was gentle of eye and slow of gesture and her admonition was mild and considerate: 'You'll do better this way.'

"To be thus publicly instructed by little girls seemed to the young scholars at first a derogation from their dignity. But since they did want to learn, they obeyed with what grace they could, and when the two girls left the twins alone, they secretly wished that their little teachers might come back and stay longer.

"In the course of the day this wish of theirs was repeatedly fulfilled. The girls came and went and came again and for the greater part of the day remained at the table of the twins. But the sons of the scribe on this day learned from the daughters of the baker not only how to pass the little cog wheels swiftly and accurately over the matzoth. They learned in addition how attractive and merry are the songs which are sung at the baking of the Paschal bread.

"Bakers are pertinacious singers, especially the younger journeymen. And particularly tireless are young Jewish bakers. By day and by night they baked. By day and by night there was singing in the house of the baker.

His children had heard the songs of the young bakers, and what they had learned in the course of the years they displayed during the baking of the Paschal bread.

"To the children of the Torah scribe, who had been brought up according to the entire sternness of the Law, singing was no profane pastime. They sang while they studied; they sang while they prayed. To them singing was study or prayer. The children of the baker sang songs of quite a different fashion, gay or sad little songs, which refresh the heart like the fragrance of fresh baked matzoth. Moreover the little girls sang in harmony, a thing which the sons of the scribe had never heard. And the way in which the two voices blended with each other enchanted the Talmud students beyond measure.

"They were most enchanted by a song which the sisters sang mockingly to the two brothers. The little song had three stanzas. The first went as follows:

> Good people who have time today,
> Active and true and pure,
> Come hither all to bake the bread,
> The matzoth of the poor.

The gentler of the two girls sang this stanza alone. Her sister undertook the second:

> Hands that are small and delicate,
> Whom all but books bring irk,
> Once in the month of Nissan try
> This rough and useful work.

In the third stanza the voices of the two girls blended:

> Sensitive children, knead the dough
> With hands the whitest seen,
> Aye, knead the dough, with prayer glow,
> Good and pure and clean.

"The boys were so pleased with this song and its gay sweet tune that they learned it on the spot and sang it repeatedly with the sisters. The patterning of the matzoth was not so much fun any more, especially since the work

59

of the children was not taken quite seriously. Even as the children used a special table, so the matzoth prepared by them were baked in a separate oven and, so soon as they were done, eaten by the children too.

"It was very late when the Torah scribe and his sons departed for home. The boys, happy and full of melodies, went over the songs which they had learned from the twin sisters on their way home, and reminded each other of a forgotten word or of a note they had missed. Before they fell asleep in their beds, Nehemiah, the older, said to Jochąnan, the younger: 'The daughters of the baker have equally lovely voices. But the name of one of them is Esther.' Jochanan said: 'Their voices are equally lovely, for they are twins. But one of them is called Rachel, and she is the younger.' "

"Next day on their way to school Jochanan, the younger, said to his older brother: 'If, instead of going into the Bakers' Alley, we were first to go around the market place and then along the Butchers' Alley, we could see the windows of the baker's house the whole time.' Nehemiah agreed earnestly with his brother's proposal. In the Bakers' Alley they would pass too closely to the baker's house; they would have had to lean back and stretch out their necks and look up at the windows. All the market women could have noticed it and nothing would have pleased them better than to gossip jeeringly concerning the two Talmud students.

"And so daily they took the detour of the market place. Facing the baker's house the boys fixed their eyes upon two particular windows, and it was not long before the daughters of the baker became aware of this daily act of homage. And daily the girls were at the window to receive this act of homage with glances and gestures of delight.

"But the market women were hardly slower than the sisters to catch on to the secret of the boys. And after the manner of market women they coupled the two pairs of twins in their gossip, even though they did not jeer. Scarcely had the brothers come into sight in the early morning in the Butchers' Alley, but that one of the market women said to her neighbor: 'There comes the pair of bridegrooms.' And before the brothers had reached the Bakers' Alley, the market women in this corner announced: 'The two brides are already at the window.'

"Daily this pantomime repeated itself on the market place. The boys came and the gossip of the market women preceded them. They went, and the gossip followed them. It was not long before the two pairs of twins were spoken of as betrothed on the tongue of the people. Everyone in the town knew it. And the girls knew it. Only the twin boys did not know it.

Thus things went for two years, and these were the happy years in the brief childhood of the twin brothers. And during these years of happiness the days of the matzoth baking were the loveliest and happiest days of their young lives.

"When the sons of the Torah scribe were twelve years old, the children of the town on the day of the matzoth baking played a gay trick upon the two sets of twins. In the innocent frolic of the occasion they feigned to celebrate the public betrothal of the twins. They made rings of dough; plates were broken and formulas pronounced. And because the ceremony of betrothal seemed too plain and simple to the children, they heightened it with teasing by blindfolding the two boys and the two girls and thus making of the ceremony the game of blind man's bluff.

"Mere chance led to Nehemiah's being paired with Rachel and Jochanan with Esther. And when the eyes of the children were uncovered, a feeling of disappointment stole into four young hearts. None of the children, however, displayed any sign of disappointment. This was easier for all four of them, since each was secretly consoled by the disappointment of the other, so that the brothers found a melancholy comfort in the disappointment of the sisters and these, reciprocally, in that of the brothers.

"The other children, however, insatiable in their

playful impulse, found the betrothal ceremonial to be too brief. In rapid understanding with each other they followed it up with a pretended wedding. A square of white linen was fastened to four long sticks and in a moment a *huppah*, a marriage canopy, was erected.

"A boy of twelve, a fellow student of the twins, played the part of the rabbi in the ceremony. He played the part so well, that the contradiction between the formal correctness of the ceremony and the ignorance of the customs of the country amused the adult observers no less than the children at their play.

"Some of these adults were so delighted with this childish imitation of a wedding ceremonial that they interposed their advice and admonitions. This well-meant interference served wholly to disrupt the ceremonial; in the height of the confusion one saw the boyish rabbi with two brides and only one bridegroom under the *huppah*.

"It was the first-born, Nehemiah, who suddenly found himself alone between the two brides under the *huppah*, the while there sounded about him the now unleashed merriment of the others. Completely withdrawn from the spirit of the game, Nehemiah stood in the midst of that wanton crowd with lowered eyes, ashamed and lost, as though a bodily pain had come upon him.

"At that moment a stranger took a hand in the game. He was a wanderer who in recent years had always appeared in the town on the day of the baking of the matzoth, quite as though an invitation had been sent him to appear. In the midst of the noisy confusion he found the lost Jochanan; he took him gently by the hand and led him under the *huppah* and thoughtfully placed him at the side not of Esther, but of the younger Rachel. And thus the crooked was made straight.

"No one observed the apparent substitution. For, though it was easy enough for anyone to distinguish between the twin sisters, yet there were only a few people in the town so keen of eye that they could distinguish between the brothers. No one observed the exchange. To

63

the children under the *huppah* the interposition of the stranger seemed a most happy accident, which corrected a most unhappy one. Now only with unshadowed soul and lightened hearts could they too have their share in the mad merriment about them.

"But when the ceremony was over and dancing and singing ensued, Jochanan took his brother aside and said to him: 'It was no accident.' Laughingly Nehemiah answered: 'All the better; you did that very well. Let us tell the sisters. They will be amused.'

" 'Neither say it nor relate it. I didn't do it. The stranger did it.' And he placed his middle finger and his little finger against his chin as students of the Talmud are wont to do when an intricate question is about to be explained. 'If the stranger did it then it was surely an accident,' Nehemiah replied, 'for how should a stranger know our secret when even here, in our community, no one knows it?'

" 'It is this very thing which frightened me. It was like this: the children held me tight; they wanted to see you under the *huppah* with two brides; they held me fast and would not let me go. I could probably have torn myself away, but I preferred not to because I had been afraid the whole time that our father might observe what was going on. Suddenly the strange man stood beside me. No one had seen him coming. He was simply there, and on the instant there was a stillness round about me.'

" 'Did the stranger frighten you?' Nehemiah asked. 'No,' Jochanan replied, 'he said no word and his face was round and mild. And yet there was this sudden silence about me. In that long silence he took me by the hand and already we were under the *huppah*. When I saw you there between Esther on your left and Rachel on your right, I took a step to the right toward Esther. A game is but a jest and in the game my bride's name is Esther, but I felt distinctly how the arm of the stranger forced me toward the left. I raised my eyes in order to see from his expression what was his meaning. At that moment he lets go of my

64

right hand; with a calm but firm grip he takes my left hand and I find myself next to Rachel. He, however, even as he suddenly appeared, so suddenly did he vanish.'

" 'Are you sure that only under the *huppah* he released your right hand and took your left?' asked Nehemiah. 'Ah yes, it was so. If I were not so sure, it would yet be an accident that he led me to Rachel, a second accident no more worth talking about than the first accident of the false betrothal. What is your opinion?'

" 'The betrothal was a game and the wedding was a game,' said Nehemiah. 'But the betrothal was stupid and the wedding lovely. Why take it so seriously? It is well that our father was not near us; he would not have permitted that kind of game and the sisters would have felt hurt. Look how merry they all are and how they dance, and Rachel is the loveliest dancer among the girls and the merriest.'

" 'If the stranger knew our secret, he is no common stranger. He has been here twice before. Both times he came on the day of the baking of the matzoth and soon thereafter departed. Who is he? He wears a coat of sheepskin as the peasants do and he uses a girdle of coarse rope as the woodcutters do. Whence does he come? Perhaps he is a hidden *Zaddik*; perhaps he is one of the thirty-six?'

" 'A secret *Zaddik*? One of the thirty-six? It may even be Elijah, the prophet, disguised as a peasant, as a woodcutter. Wonders seem nowadays to be in every street! Had the stranger been one of the thirty-six, he would not have taken you first by the right hand and then by the left; he would have known your place from the beginning.'

"Jochanan regarded his brother with radiant eyes. He delighted in Nehemiah's acuteness and the swiftness of his thinking which was a source of daily pleasure and astonishment to the teacher and the fellow students in their school. 'You are right,' said he. 'It was an accident.' And with eased minds the brothers were able to join the other children in their games. They danced with those who danced and sang with those who sang.

65

"It was shortly before midnight when the Torah scribe left the bake house with his sons and went toward his house. The night was cold and clear by the gleam of the new moon and the stars. In a sharp wind the icicles under the eaves tinkled. The slender sickle of the moon and the stars seemed gray and cold as though made of ice.

"The children, heated by their play, shivered. Swiftly they walked on the crunching snow and now and then the old Torah scribe lingered behind them on the snowy road. As they passed by the synagogue, they saw light in one of the vestibules. With their candles a few old men sat over their books, but one could see that they were not studying but praying. These were *hasidim* and students of the Cabala who arise at midnight and get up from their beds and, whether in their own houses alone or in the vestibule of a House of Prayer together, recite *hatzot*, that is to say, prayers of mourning over the exile of Israel.

"Outside of the synagogue, in front of the lit window, there was a man who hopped up and down in the square of snow illuminated by the light. Whenever he hopped near that lit window in order to peer in, the children could see the man quite clearly. Everything about him was round: his head, his forehead, his nose, his chin. And his whole body in fact, wrapped in his sheepskin coat, and held by a rope, was as round as a little keg. Although he was standing in front of that window in frost and in snow, he kept raising the back of his hand to his forehead and patting his forehead, as though it were hot and perspiring. 'Why, that's the stranger, the Round One,' Jochanan whispered to his brother. 'Yes, and round as a ball he is,' said Nehemiah. The stranger turned around, as though he had been called by name. Then he turned away from the window and spat repeatedly on the snow.

" 'The poor man,' said the Torah scribe, 'he is of a sickly fatness and not quite right in his head.' The children wanted to know why their father thought the round fat man was not in his right mind, and Nehemiah asked him. The Torah scribe looked for a while toward the man at the window and then said as though to himself: 'Even in the bake house and by bright daylight he said more than once "Bake your matzoth. Bake your matzoth quickly. It is late; it is late." We thought him a little mad then. But he seems to be really crazy, the poor man. Come, children.' Now the scribe went ahead and the children followed him. Before they lost sight of the Round One, they heard him say in a thin, nasal voice: 'They get up at midnight . . . They weep over the exiled *Shekhinah* . . . For them it is never too late . . . They are crazy; Pfui!' "

"This evening was the last evening on which the children of the Torah scribe were together with the children of the baker in a spirit of merriment and joy. For after that Paschal feast the scribe saw the time at hand to prepare his sons, who were entering their thirteenth year, to be each one a *Bar Mitzvah* and thus enter into the community of Israel. Since he himself was a *Kohen* and his sons *Kohanim* by birth it would soon be time too to initiate them into the service of the *Kohanim*. With that the days of their childhood and the games of their boyhood came to an end.

"In the week just before Shavuoth Jochanan said one morning to his brother: 'Perhaps we should stop taking the roundabout way across the market place and looking up at the baker's windows. We are *Kohanim* and we should cease doing whatever will be imputed as a sin to us when we have reached thirteen.'

"Nehemiah agreed and from this morning on until the day of their doom the twin brothers did not see their friends again. It was not easy for them to deny themselves the daily habit which had become so dear. But they had grown up from their earliest childhood in so deep a veneration of the *Kohanic* service, that they resisted the daily temptation without ever again speaking of the renunciation which they had laid upon themselves.

"Well did the brothers remember the first holy shiver of their childhood when for the first time, they had heard all the *Kohanim* of the city pronounce the priestly blessing over the community in prayer. They had heard them, not seen them, for no sooner had the *Kohanim* mounted the Almemor, scarcely had they drawn over their faces the silver-embroidered tops of their prayer shawls and raised their arms on high, when a fearful whispering passed from mouth to mouth of the younger generation of worshipers and warned them: Do not look upon the hands of the *Kohanim*! While they are blessing the people the *Shekhinah* descends upon their hands. He who looks upon them loses the light of his eyes, forever dazzled by the radiance of the *Shekhinah*.

"The frightened children hid their faces in the prayer books and the chanting of the *Kohanim* sounded above the bowed heads of the worshipers, like a rain of words and tones, now soft, now strong, a consolation blended of force and light—a blessing. And they heard the voice of their father who was, among these speaking and singing pronouncers of a blessing, the chanter and intoner. How they would like to have raised their heads and looked up!

"When they had been seven, Nehemiah had once confessed to his brother, how he had not been able to resist the temptation. Out of the corner of an eye he had furtively glanced up at the *Kohanim*. And yet he had not been stricken with blindness. Frightened more by this confession than by the breach of law itself, the boys had gone to their father and told him. The Torah scribe had smiled kindly and had said to Nehemiah: 'Because you are yourself a *Kohen*, your curiosity was interpreted as a desire for knowledge and so forgiven. Our sages say: "The over-modest cannot well learn." On the other hand we are warned against rashness and impatience. There is a time for everything, for asking as well as for learning.'

"Now that each was ripe to be a *Bar Mitzvah*, they were permitted to know everything that was not hidden lore, and they did not restrain their questioning. 'Why do the *Kohanim* raise their arms on high?' Jochanan wanted to know. 'In the first of the five books, in the fourth section, our arch-father Abraham said: "And I raise up my hands to God, to the El Elyon," ' the Torah scribe explained. 'And why do the *Kohanim* spread out their fingers in their blessing?' asked Nehemiah. 'In *Shemoth*, the Book of Exodus, in the ninth section, Moses, our teacher, says: "I will spread out my hands unto the Creator," ' the scribe instructed them. 'And why do the *Kohanim* hold their fingers so that two of them on one side and two of them on the other, together with the thumb, form the letter *Shin?*' both boys desired to know. 'Because the letter *Shin* is the first letter of the pronounceable name of the Ineffable, namely, *Shaddai*,' the scribe explained. And Nehemiah with lowered eyes added an explanation of his own to this one: 'The word *Shekhinah* also begins with the letter *Shin*, wherefore it is forbidden to the *Kohanim* themselves to look upon their hands raised in blessing, because the radiance of the *Shekhinah* is upon those hands.'

"The twins were zealous in asking and continuing to ask. Not rarely did one of them put a question which a Talmud student might well himself have elucidated. And that was because in the course of the daily instruction the sons learned how deeply happy their questions made their father; and they rivaled each other in questioning so as to prolong the hours of instruction.

" 'There is so much talk of war nowadays,' Nehemiah said to his father, and at once added the question: 'In ancient times were there so many wars and so many battles as in our time?' 'No,' said the scribe, 'in ancient times there was not so much war nor so much shedding of blood as in our time. For as the warlike nations invent more and deadlier weapons, they make war more frequently against each other.'

" 'But if in olden times the peoples made war against each other less often, why were our people always so concerned over peace?' Jochanan asked and continued by say-

70

ing: 'Our books are full of prayers for peace and songs of peace. Our most sacred blessings, the blessings of the *Kohanim*, are blessings of peace. And all over the world, wherever a Jew meets another, he greets him with the greeting of peace and says. "Shalom, peace be with you." Why is this so?'

" 'The word *Shalom*, peace, is derived from the word *Shalem*, and this word signifies: whole, unharmed, unoppressed, perfect. Our prayers, when they invoke peace, and our songs, when they praise peace, assuredly include in meaning that peace which is the contrary of war. But these blessings and greetings, when they use the word *Shalom* mean peace between yourself and your brother, between yourself and your neighbor, between yourself and every human being, between yourself and every living thing, between yourself and the whole of creation.' This was the explanation which the Torah scribe gave to his sons.

"And although this explanation of the word *Shalom* quite satisfied his sons, yet after further reflection the scribe added: 'The greeting *Shalom*, however, means first of all: May peace be unto you and peace within you. Let there be no disunity within you, no struggle between your soul and your body, no division between your thought and your act. For the kind of wisdom which asserts that there is a split and a conflict between the soul and the body of man, is the false wisdom of the heathen. They, the heathen, assert that the body is the unclean vessel of the soul, in order thus to justify the unruly wilfulness of their spirit. True for us is the teaching of the prayer: "The soul is Thine, the body is Thine; have mercy upon Thy work." '

"The scribe enjoyed these hours as the unexpected boon of his old age. Every evening he sat in his study, Nehemiah at his right hand, and Jochanan at his left, and all three chanted the responsory verses of the blessing, the boys with arms raised high and spread out hands, the father with his hands over the prayer book, singing the

blessing, word after word, with tireless devotion and thereupon listening in ecstasy to the singing of his sons, as it
soared upward.

"Thus passed the evenings of the summer. The Torah scribe, absorbed by his belated paternal joys, had long
forgotten the warning which had once been addressed to
him. He forgot even the fact of his forgetfulness. He forgot himself and the world and the great woe that was in
the world. For a long time now had the great war been
raging in the West of the continent and the sorrow of the
Jews became the sorrow of the other peoples; it became
the true sorrow of the world.

"At the eleventh hour there came another warning
to the scribe. One early evening, while he was rehearsing
the blessings of peace with his sons, there arose in the
frame of the open window the outline of a foreign old man
who had, once or twice before, standing at some distance
from the house, listened to the chanting and had attracted
the attention of the children by his attitude of fear and
his special way of listening. For a while he looked straight
into the face of the scribe with his sad and frightened
eyes. Then he wished them all a good evening and added
quickly and in very faulty Yiddish: 'You don't recognize
me, Zacharia, and it is just as well. For it is not important
whether you speak to me or not. All I care about is that
you should listen to me for a little while and follow my
advice without any delay and any reflection. The danger
is great. It is near and it is deadly. I speak to you in the
presence of your children, because I want to frighten you
in their presence and them in yours. I want to frighten you
and your children and all who are of our faith. Nothing
but terror can save us, and our terror cannot be great
enough. For great as it may be, the danger that threatens
us is even greater, far greater and deadlier. It is a danger
that can be meted with no human measure.

" 'Here you and your children chant the blessings
of peace! Let the chanting be and see to it that you and
yours escape! In the Name of the Creator of the world, see

to your escape! Flee as swiftly as possible. Whither? I know not whither. I only know the direction. It must be eastward. For what comes from the West no man, who is worthy of being a man, will survive.'

" 'You should know,' said the scribe, grasping the hands of his frightened children. 'Who should know but you? You made your pact with the West, with the enlightened West and all its superstition. You want to inspire fear in—us? I recall the days when you had nothing but jeering and disgust for all our Jewish fears, which you contemned and trod under your feet as Jewish fears.'

" 'So you do recognize me,' said the old man and the mourning in his eyes became more intense. 'You do recognize me and you are now minded to recall my sins to us both. Spare me that, Zacharia, and spare yourself. For they are minded to tear up our people root and branch. They have become capable of anything. They have all the weapons and we have nothing, nothing but our blind equanimity, our thoughtlessness, and also the jeers of the pagan world. We have but a single weapon and the name of it is—survival. Arise! Flee and save yourselves! Did not the angel say to Ezra: "The survivors are far more blessed than those who have died?" '

" 'To Ezra, as *we* read him, the angel said a different thing. You tell me that they have all weapons and we have nothing? We have our faith. It is your opinion that I am to leave off chanting the blessings of peace and run away? That blessing of ours will survive them and all their wars and all their victories. I am to run away? This coming week we celebrate those Holy Days which we call the Days of Awe. On those days the fate of the world is decided. What will be decided for the world and for my people, that is true for me too. You seek to frighten me and my children? I and my house will remain faithful to the Eternal. Did he frighten you, Nehemiah?' 'No,' said Nehemiah in a strong voice. 'Did he frighten you, Jochanan?' 'No,' whispered Jochanan in a feeble voice.

" 'The Days of Awe are coming,' the old man con-

tinued. 'I tell you, Zacharia, that frightful days are coming. Blood will drip from the trees and the stones will cry
out. The tyrant of the end of days has appeared. The German messiah with his Aryan lie! It is well for you, Zacharia, that you have faith and confidence. But history
teaches us that God does not bar the way of the wicked.'

" 'It is not our history which teaches us thus, Gedalia
ben Yitzhak. Go your own way. If it lead you to security
and escape, all the better for you. But your way is not my
way.' With these words the Torah scribe arose and went
to the open window and closed it before the old man
whose countenance was full of consternation.

"But the old man was not affronted. For quite a
while he remained by the closed window, as though to
indicate that he still had much to say. Not until he was
persuaded that he was lingering in vain, did he spread
out his arms in a gesture of compassionate adjuration,
turn hesitantly away and go off slowly, as though weighed
down by his own dismay.

" 'Who is he?' Jochanan asked. 'Once upon a time
his name was Gedalia and he was the very pride of our
Yeshivah. But in early youth errors distracted him and
he migrated to the West. A *meshumad*!' said the Torah
scribe. 'For decades we had no news of him. Then, a year
ago, he turned up here once more, a broken man. He lives
with his sister.' 'How can he be a *meshumad*,' Jochanan
asked excitedly, 'since he said: "of our faith"?' In some
astonishment the scribe looked from Jochanan to Nehemiah: 'Did he really say that? Did you, too, hear it?'
Scarcely had his brother replied affirmatively when Jochanan, without waiting for his father to approve, hastily
ran out of the door and overtook the old man.

" 'Sir,' Jochanan said, the while the old man
stretched out both hands to the excited lad, 'peace be with
you, Reb Gedalia,' he corrected himself and laid his own
right hand into the right hand of the old man. 'Peace,
peace,' the old man stammered, no less excited than the
boy. 'Peace be with you, my son. But do not address me

as Reb Gedalia; I do not deserve it.' 'But you are of our faith?' said Jochanan. 'Assuredly, assuredly,' said the old man. 'I have committed many sins, but I am not a renegade. Tell your father that, my dear boy; do, and at once.' 'Yes,' said Jochanan, 'I will do it at once.'

"'Wait, my child. Tell your father that I have spoken with a commander from among the Reds. Tell your father that the roads to the East are open to any who would save themselves. Tell your father further that we will have a vehicle for myself and my sister. Tell him furthermore that in that vehicle there will be place for all of you, all four. And tell your father that we are leaving at dawn tomorrow.'

"Breathlessly Jochanan gave his father the old man's message. The scribe heard it with joy. So it was not true. The friend of his youth, Gedalia Brandweiner, once the pride of a *Yeshivah*, had certainly gone upon aberrant ways and in the great world of the West had achieved fame in some of the arts of those lands under the name of Georg Brandt. But he was no renegade, no *meshumad*. The rest of the message the father heard with but half an ear.

"Upon that evening Reb Zacharia did not resume the chanting with his two small *Kohanim*. The succeeding days he passed, as did all the pious, in preparation and expectation of those Holy Days which are called the Days of Awe. But on the eve of Rosh Hashanah doom descended on our city: the first armored cars of the Germans appeared at the River Seret."

"During that night we heard the tumult of battle. And when at the very break of day we ventured out into the street we saw the victors of those nocturnal skirmishes crowd into the city. There were the Germans in their grayish-green uniforms and on their sleeves were the hooked crosses, the swift pockmarks of the German pestilence.

"On that day of their rapid victory they did us almost no harm. Perhaps it was that these soldiers were no murderers; perhaps it was that they wanted to give no respite to the fleeing Reds and so had no time for murder. The bloody deeds of this day and of those that followed were committed by our fellow citizens, our neighbors. Ah, it is an ancient sorrow that in the days of their history, whether fortunate or wretched, it was always they, our neighbors, who were prone to vent their spleen on us. That is an old story, a European and Christian refrain.

"And yet, contemptible as they were, what were the deeds of violence of our neighbors compared to the ill deeds of the German murderers, as they now set in? Those were raging flames; these were all-consuming forest fires. Those neighbors devoured hundreds of us, but millions were spared. These others devoured millions and only hundreds were saved.

"I, the narrating judge, mournfully name the deeds

of violence of our neighbors, inspired more by the lust of gain than by the lust of blood, in order to commemorate those victims too, may their names be sanctified. Concerning the misdeeds of the German murderers the accusing judge will soon bear witness, and he will do so according to the measure of the blood guiltiness, primarily of the blood guiltiness incurred upon the bodies and lives of our children: from the newborn to those of thirteen; that is to say, children according to our Law.

"May the accusing judge be upheld before this court by the merits of our fathers and the memory of our martyrs who fell for the Sanctification of the Name. And may strength be granted him to speak of what is unspeakable, that is, to bear witness according to the needs of this court, not to delineate, for that would be contrary to our Law. For only he could succeed in describing these bloody deeds and delineate them who was in a measure allied to the monsters who committed them. Only such a one would be willing and capable of rehearsing these deeds in word or writing or image.

"Now the accusation could begin. But I perceive that a judge has not yet assumed his seat. Where is the seventh judge?" "The seventh seat was destined for Zacharia Hakohen, the Torah scribe." Thus spoke the *Ab Beth-Din*, the leading judge. "But he seems to be delaying. Since danger is imminent, another judge must serve as a substitute." "What danger do you see in a delay?" asked the narrating judge. "The procedure must not be interrupted," said the *Ab Beth-Din*, "because a Higher Court, as we know from the Messenger, is waiting for the result of these proceedings. This publican will take the seventh seat as a substitute judge." Therewith he pointed to the taciturn one among the publicans and said to him: "Reb Senderl ben Hayim, the water carrier, known as Havryluk the publican, you have been found worthy to sit on this court as the seventh judge and to pass judgment."

This appointment came upon the taciturn publican with such grievousness, that he had to hold on to the arm of the Messenger in order not to faint on the stairs. Then he broke into sobs and lamented aloud in order to be heard by the other judges on the Almemor. And in his lamentation he accused himself: "I have denied the Name of the Creator. For four years I have not lived according to the Law. For four years I hid myself under the name of Havryluk when the true Havryluk disappeared. I wanted to live, rather live under a false name than die with my brethren. And now I am to be a judge, I?"

"You have not denied the Name of the Lord, Senderl ben Hayim," the Messenger consoled him. "You have denied only your own name. You have pretended to be Havryluk and you were believed. It is well. For you live, and that is well. More grace is upon the living than upon the dead. Otherwise you would not have been alive. And as for the name of Havryluk—it is a beautiful name, for Havryluk is derived from Havrilo and that is a form of the name Gabriel. It is a good name. Look upon me; my name, too, is Gabriel. And the name displeases neither the Lord nor me. Do you imagine that Senderl is a better or a purer name than Gabriel?"

"No, no," said the water carrier, "I do not believe that." "Very well, then," said the Messenger; "your answer is one that will be pleasing everywhere. And now you will bend down and lift up the box. You will carry it to the wall on which the pictures are painted. And you will lay it down at the feet of the smaller of the two images, so that it will remain clearly in the sight of the judges."

"How am I to lift up the box and carry it all by myself, seeing that five strong men were unable to budge it?" Senderl the water carrier lamented. But he wept no more, for fear had gone from him. "You brought it hither," said the Messenger; "Have you forgotten that?"

"It was two of us who brought it here, the oldest of the publicans and I," said Senderl, "Do you not know it?" "I know it well," said the Messenger. "But to the oldest of the publicans another task has been assigned. Did you not observe that it was he who, during the narration of the

78

story about the Torah scribe and his twin sons, led the judges from the subterranean passage here, one after another? He is now seeking for the Torah scribe. Therefore you will carry the box alone. Do it and ask no further."

The water carrier bent low over the box, placed both of his arms about its middle and lifted it with such obvious ease, that all, except the Messenger, were speechless with astonishment. But the officer of the storm troopers stretched out an arm toward the box with a gesture as though to ward off a thing of horror and thrice stammered the words: "A shrine, a shrine, a shrine." "You found your tongue again at almost the right time," said the Messenger to the officer. "You will soon need to use it." "I am innocent," the officer stammered. "I have acted as I was ordered to do. That is my job. I am a soldier." "The court will decide in that matter," said the Messenger.

The water carrier, Senderl, equally astonished at the lightness of the box, kept it in happy surprise in the crook of his left arm, while his right hand caressed the wood. He said to the Messenger: "It is as light as . . . as . . ." "As what?" the Messenger helped his faltering speech. "Say it, just say it," he encouraged him. "I was going to say that it is as light as a Torah scroll," the water carrier said with his delighted glance steadfastly on the box. "Those are wise and good words, Reb Senderl," the Messenger commended him. "If you will then carry it to the place where it belongs, you will not find it difficult to think of and to say the right thing in the court and to join in its decisions. Go and neglect nothing."

The water carrier who, for four long years, had lived disguised and so in constant fear of being discovered and betrayed and, like all his brothers, subjected to torture, now faced yet another danger, namely, of smiling with joy with that box against his bosom. But he had the strength to withstand this temptation too, and broke out in tears instead.

With unguarded face, weeping as effortlessly as a child, he carried the box as he had been bidden to the

79

painted wall of the old synagogue and placed it length-
wise at the feet of the smaller of the two figures. But when
he perceived that the box, standing thus on end, corresponded exactly to the measure of that smaller figure, he
stopped weeping, again consoled as easily as a child. With
lowered head, as though opposing himself to a violent
wind, he trod swiftly to the Almemor, mounted the narrow steps that led to it and reached his place on the bench
at the very moment in which the prosecutor's accusation
began.

"On the eve of Yom Kippur new troops penetrated our city. This was a species of soldiery such as the history of the world has not seen; such as the history of the world will never see again—unless, in truth, humanity in blasphemous self-forgetfulness ever again permits that people to raise its blood-drenched head.

"Their entrance into the town was accompanied by a wild whirl of drums, a mad shrilling of pipes and a coarse ditty of murder, assassination and shameless delight in blood-sprent knives. The music might have reminded one of the hoarse braying of the Janissaries, had one not been forced at once to remember that even those savage hordes, compared to these troops, would have seemed a well-bred community of knights.

"These troops had been specifically trained for deeds of violence against the defenceless; they had been drilled to commit rapine and murder and torture. They were called by two German words which meant Protective Echelons and were called according to the German initials of those two words: the S.S.! Thus and not otherwise will we call them here. For no other name so sinister, no other sound so impure, could ever fall to the depth of unspeakable shame in which those two hissing letters will forever dwell in the horrified memory of mankind! S.S.—the Soilers of the Source, the defilers of Creation.

"In order to deceive us and to illustrate the neo-Nordic ethics of treachery, the S.S. did not behave worse on the eve of Yom Kippur than any other horde of mercenaries drunk with victory. They fed, they guzzled, they sang their vulgar songs and, restrained by no shame or discipline, went hunting for women in the open streets.

"Sundry of their leaders, in fact, amused themselves by visiting the old synagogue during the chanting of the *Kol Nidrei*. With them were heavily armed troopers, but these they left behind them outside of the door. Standing on the steps they listened in well-mannered fashion to the chanting of our cantor and his boys' choir. And the *Kol Nidrei* pleased these strange visitors so well that they cried out, demanding a repetition of the chant. We thought at first they did this out of the coarseness of their ignorance. They did it, however, in order to degrade us and our prayers.

"While the cantor, following a desperate gesture of the old Rav, repeated the prayer in a voice touched with shame, one of these visitors made sketches on a block of paper and also took photographs with an apparatus that clicked and emitted a flame both hissing and dazzling. It was the same infamous art rogue who was later to paint the murals on that wall.

"After the *Kol Nidrei* had been repeated these creatures clapped in excessive applause with their unclean hands. Then, accompanied by the tumult of arms, they went out, even as they had come. They left us to our prayers; they left us in the melancholy hope of being able to survive this Day of Judgment without further desecration.

"We stayed in the synagogue all that Yom Kippur night. With our wives and our children we passed that night in prayer and in terror. And the night seemed astonishingly short to us. We experienced for the first time the fact that deadly terror contracts time. Between prayers we reminded ourselves—and this recollection consoled us —of the days of the First World War, when our town was occupied by Austrian troops. On that occasion, too, we had

82

guests during the Kol Nidrei prayer. A number of officers of the occupying army visited us during that hour too. They were Christian soldiers and they stood on that very stair in friendly and even reverent attitudes and listened to the chanting. 'These Germans are Christians too; at least on Yom Kippur they will let us fast and pray in peace.' Thus we consoled ourselves and persuaded ourselves that we were safe and in God's hand.

"When morning came it seemed as though the Creator had heard our prayers. None came back that morning. Nor were any of them seen in the Jewish quarter, nor did we hear anything about them until the ending of *Shaharit*, the morning prayer, which takes up the whole forenoon on Yom Kippur.

"Toward one o'clock—the scroll of the Torah had just been unrolled and the reader stood at the lectern on the Almemor—Christian children appeared and told our children that the Germans had driven the Jews of the nearby villages and smaller settlements into the little forest near the town where, surrounded by armed peasants and mounted machine guns, they were digging trenches and bunkers.

"Our Rav took counsel with Reb Moshe Parnas, who was a substitute mayor of our city. And we sent a delegation of three men, headed by Reb Moshe, to the Christian mayor with the request that he might plead for the village Jews and, perhaps, too, with the help of the Christian priests, effect their liberation from the Germans.

"The three suppliants went in their Yom Kippur garb, their prayer shawls wrapped around their white shrouds. Hastily they had put their shoes on over their white socks. Their faces were almost as white as their garments but their tread was swift and strong, like the tread of those who set out to be of help to their brothers in a time of need.

"The three set out toward the city hall before the reading of the Torah portion, and although the way to the city hall was very short, they had not returned after the reading of the Torah portion had been completed. It seemed permissible to our Rav under the circumstances to delay the praying of *Mussaf* for a space. There were more than four thousand of us in the synagogue on that long day, men, women, children. We waited during a silent hour. Then we took refuge in our prayers again. We raised our voices and cried out, all of us, men, and women, and children. For even the youngest of us had the premonition that we were dedicated to death.

"At the decline of the day, when we were praying the prayers of *Neilah*, the ending prayers of Yom Kippur, sustained by a last hope, our friend, the publican Andrej, came to us and told the worshipers who were standing on the stair by the entrance: 'Your three emissaries will not come back. On the way to the courthouse they fell into the hands of a squad of S.S. men. With jeers and contempt they were driven along the main street of the town and thereafter into the municipal forest where the village Jews are . . .' 'Where the village Jews *were*,' he said, as though to correct an error. 'For they are no more, these village Jews. They did not dig trenches, as we supposed. What they dug all morning was a great hole, a mass grave, their own grave. For after they had finished their digging they were separated into rows and groups in such formation that those who had not yet been murdered had to throw those who had been mowed down by the machine guns into this grave, before it was their own turn to be shot down. Of the many thousands the murderers spared only a few hundred, vigorous men and women, whom they are now loading into cattle cars at the railroad station. Of children, there were none left alive.'

"To our eternal grief and to the grief of all who still breathe, let it be said, that those who heard this thing, namely, our brothers on that stair, would not have this thing to be true. More, they resented so harshly the tragic message of the good messenger who brought it, that that good friend first hid his face in his hands and in his speechless consternation ran on to the smaller houses of prayer where he hoped to find credence.

"And because our brothers on the stair refused to believe the message, they suppressed it instantly. And they closed the gate to the synagogue, even as they had closed their ears. And so the message concerning the village Jews, even as those Jews themselves, preceded us unheard to death.

"The sun was sinking at the ending of the day and our fast was coming to an end and the prayers were coming to an end. With a last flaming of his voice the cantor had just beseechingly sung those great words: *'P'tach lanu shaar*—open a gate to our prayers,' when sharp rifle reports interrupted the prayer and the gate of the synagogue was crashed open. The S.S. were upon us.

"As though those first shots had slain them as they rose from our lips, our prayers fell into silence. The silence was so deep that the gentle hissing of the innumerable memorial candles guttering in the sand boxes to their extinction, smote upon us like the roaring of a forest fire. Muffled in our white prayer shawls, petrified by sudden fright, each himself a pale candle of death, we stood there unshod, men in prayer, men fasting. Beyond, on that stair, armed to the teeth, stood they, the assassins.

"The old Rav was the first who stirred. He put his prayer book and his spectacles on the lectern; he drew his prayer shawl tightly about his aged form; with arms raised in beseeching he strode toward the intruders. They let him come. When he had reached the stair he bowed deeply before the young leader of the S.S., as before a king. 'Let us end our prayers on this Day of Atonement, on this Day of Judgment!' he pleaded and bowed still deeper, so deep that his high forehead almost touched the stone of the stair. 'The day of requital,' that murderous youngster jeered and shot thrice—into the head, the neck, the back of the Rav.

"Rabbi Shimeon ben Yehudah Halevy, whose blood the Eternal will avenge, was the first to fall in this synagogue. His soul was gentle, pious, saintly. Why such a man had to die in this manner—of that we are not competent to judge. That it was not granted him to breathe his last with the cry: *Sh'ma Yisrael*, is not to be understood by us. But that he had to breathe his last here, in this House, during *Neilah*, with words upon his lips which defiled those lips, in the language of his murderer, must be attributed to an error of Heaven."

"That is sheer blasphemy!" the younger priest cried out in a loud voice. In order to calm him the older priest said to the Messenger: "We are mere witnesses here, as you, Messenger, told us. But even as mere witnesses we must notify you of our objection." The Messenger's reply was gentle: "That you are mere witnesses you have yourselves said. You are still at liberty to join this court as judges. Decide at once, for danger is ahead."

In rapid whispers the priests consulted each other and the older of them addressed the Messenger: "We do not feel called upon to sit in judgment here and we must also refuse to act as witnesses. If our presence here is not considered an accident we are prepared to lend our presence, one as an expert, the other as an observer."

"The court accepts this proposal," the *Ab Beth-Din*, the presiding judge, at once proclaimed, and added: "Nevertheless, I warn you that only the expert will be permitted to speak. The observer must remain silent. What was it that the expert desired to express?" "In my character of expert," the younger priest answered, "I merely repeat my objection to an expression of the prosecutor which I regard as blasphemous."

"What is the precise meaning of the word blasphemy?" the *Ab Beth-Din* asked the narrating judge who at once gave a brief explanation: "Blasphemy means: *Hillul Hashem*—Desecration of the Name." The *Ab Beth-Din* reflected no longer and said: "If blasphemy is interpreted as *Hillul Hashem* we have heard nothing from the accuser that can be so interpreted. What the accuser said was no part of his accusation. It was rather a lament. This court will hear not only the accusation and the defense. With his accusation the accuser will also continue his lamentation. And this lamentation was a prayer—a prayer to Heaven against Heaven—a prayer of indignation. This court encourages such prayers. The unheard of has come to pass. We will hear the unheard of in this place. It is late, almost too late. Let the accuser continue."

"The three shots which laid low our Rav were the signal shots of coldly planned murder. For suddenly the lethal fire set in from all sides. The S.S. fired with their machine guns from the stair. With lashes and gun butts they drove the women and children from their gallery down into the Hall of Prayer and set up their machine guns in the women's gallery too.

"Peasants who had been armed by the S.S. with rifles and pistols shot through the windows into the thronged Hall of Prayer. They shot in blind rage. They needed not to take aim. Wherever a bullet flew into the Hall of Prayer it hit a forehead, a breast, a body, a heart, a man, a woman, a child, a life.

"The mortally wounded had no place to fall. They bled to death in the arms of those who had not yet been wounded. They fell across the lecterns, across the sand boxes with their commemorative candles and, here and there, their blood extinguished a candle. The cries of death rose so high that they rose above the rattle and the crackling of the shooting.

"No one can say how long this lasted. Suddenly the firing ceased at some command. A voice, magnified by a loud speaker, roared down to us from the women's gallery. 'This is only a reminder!' the high-pitched, strident voice screamed. 'We will teach the Jews to respect the regulations of the German army. This is a battle territory. Political assemblies are forbidden. These Jewish cheats, however, act as though they are praying and hold political meetings in all synagogues. The S.S. are not to be taken in by such trickery.' The voice at the loud speaker shrieked many other vilifications and wild insults. Finally it gave the order that we were to be divided into two groups: men at the right; women and children at the left; a clear passageway through the middle.

"Even in this hour we tried to hope that these monsters in a last stirring of humanity would spare our women and children. And so we hastened to carry out this command. Our haste did not suffice the S.S.: they fired at us in order to increase our haste. Now they took aim. Their bullets hit a son who was bending over a dying father or a mother who lingered over a dying son.

"Still nurturing the hope that they would spare our women and children, we gathered in two groups. But the S.S. men were concerned only about the uncluttered passageway which they desired to have as broad and clean as possible. They wanted a sufficing distance between us and themselves. Our white garments of Yom Kippur were flecked with the blood of our brothers. The hands of the S.S. men were clean.

"Scarcely had the broad passage been cleared, when they came marching down the steps in two columns. They were not all identically armed. One had a pistol and a whip, another a rifle with fixed bayonet; the weapons in their hands were ready to shoot, to thrust, to strike.

"There were about twenty men in each of the two columns. The one column formed a line facing the men, the other an equal line facing the women and children. They accomplished this formation in tumultuous haste and at a military trot. Even during that trot they began to examine our rows.

"A mustering out took place. Each of the S.S. men, when he found among us a man or a woman, young and

89

vigorous enough for forced labor, would separate such an one from our midst and drive him with the others through the passage and up the stairs and out of the door. Whoever did not swiftly enough follow this command was treated to a lash of the whip, a blow of a gun butt or a kick with the boot. A young mother who wanted to take along her two-year-old child was threatened by an S.S. man with a pistol aimed not at her, but at the child.

"Since this mustering out was accomplished by forty men, the decisions between life and death took place swiftly. The empty passageway grew broader and broader and our own columns became thin. We could now have counted our dead, had we been given time.

"Yet the S.S. were not to succeed in carrying out their action quite as planned. There occurred an amazing incident. Such is their version. *We* declare it to have been a crime and horror so unspeakable that even the S.S. men sought later to deny it. It gave the S.S. bloody game of that Yom Kippur an unanticipated turn.

"As the narrating judge has told us, there lived in this town two pairs of twins, the sons of the Torah scribe and the daughters of the baker, who since their earliest years had been united by a childlike love. To Nehemiah and Jochanan this Yom Kippur had been a day of special significance. They had attained their thirteenth year. For the first time they were permitted to join their elders in the long day's fast. For the first time had they stood with the other *Kohanim* on the Almemor and had sung the choral blessing of the priests over Israel. That Yom Kippur had therefore been a day of special meaning also for Esther and Rachel, the twelve-year-old twin daughters of the baker.

"As we have also heard, these four children had not met since the evening of the baking of the matzoth. Nor did they on that Yom Kippur see each other until the decline of the day and the final prayers. The sons of the Torah scribe prayed uninterruptedly with the adults and were careful, on this Day of Atonement, not to revert in their thoughts to the holidays of childhood, when they had joined the other children and also the daughters of the baker in front of the synagogue.

"But it seems as though the twins were destined to meet again in the hour of dread and death. Whether they had sought each other out, no one knows. People asserted that the wife of the Torah scribe had taken the daughters of the baker with her to the women's gallery, so that they might look down into the hall where the men were praying, because the wife of the baker had no seat in the first row from which one could use the windows that gave on the hall below.

"However that may be, the two mothers and the twin children had been observed standing up and together before the murdering had begun. Only after the horrors set in and the division into two groups took place, did one of the children get lost. It was the smallest of them, the girl Rachel. Jochanan, who had held her hand in his during the tumult, told her mother how Rachel had suddenly torn her hand away and with a cry rushed to her father whom Jochanan too, for an instant, had seen bending over his lectern. The two mothers and the three children peered and peered to find them. But they saw neither Rachel nor her father.

"It was not until our lines had grown thin through the mustering out that Jochanan saw his little friend. Her father no longer stood beside her. The baker was dying when the child sought refuge with him. The mother cried out to her: Jochanan offered to go fetch her. But the S.S. man in this section drove him back among the women.

"The mother plucked up all her courage and approached the S.S. man and begged and besought him to be so kind as to let her fetch her child. 'Where did she go to?' the S.S. man asked in a friendly and helpful tone. 'There she is, the little girl in the white dress,' Jochanan informed the man, since the mother was in tears, being so moved by the helpfulness of the S.S. man. 'The lassie prefers the

91

menfolks,' the S.S. man said in his comfortable South German dialect. 'I'll fetch the lassie for you!'

"With broad, tranquil tread, as though he were walking across a freshly mown meadow, his rifle with fixed bayonet in his great peasant's fist, he traversed the breadth of the middle passage in the direction where the girl Rachel stood, petrified by terror and grief, over the body of her father. One or two paces from the child the S.S. man wound his other fist over the butt of his rifle. He gave a brief thrust, ran the bayonet through the bosom of the child, lifted her up and with that same slow, comfortable tread he returned across the passage, his gun with the bayoneted child bleeding high in the air.

"Everyone, the light of whose eyes was not extinguished by this sight, remembered the tread of that S.S. man. His comrades looked on with grins. But the mustering out process was interrupted. When he had reached the spot where the mother of the victim had fallen into a faint, the S.S. man lowered his gun above her and let the dead child slide with precision onto the lap of the mother. Then he said: 'Now the whole *mishpoche* is nicely united.'

" 'You . . . murderer . . . German! The lightning will slay you!' Jochanan cried into the creature's face. The S.S. man, as though hardly trusting his own ears, listened with astonished eyes to the boy's voice. Then he swung the butt of his gun high.

"And now the thing happened. Someone—and to this day one knows not who—spat into the murderer's face in a precise arc. The spittle hit the man between the eyes. The swinging rifle fell from his fists. With a cry: 'My face is burning up!' the assassin crashed on the floor. Three S.S. men hastened forward and tried to lift him up. But when they saw his face which had been burned crisply to the very bone, they too took fright and let him lie.

"After a brief consultation one of them went to the commander, who stood on the top of the stair and in the twilight of the evening could not clearly oversee the bloody goings on. Another S.S. man who had been near the dead culprit recognized Jochanan and going near him ran his bayonet through him. Jochanan fell down next to Rachel. He had been standing above her. A game of childhood had betrothed them; death wedded them forever.

"While the commander of the S.S. and his immediate comrades marched through the stillness, broken only by the rattle of their weapons, there arose in the northeast corner of the Hall of Prayer a calm, deep voice and, audible to all, said in Hebrew: 'Extinguish the lights!' "

"The remnants of hundreds of candles flickered in the sand boxes. But we still had breath enough to blow them out. In an instant the Hall of Prayer was in utter darkness. In another instant our two groups were in movement and the women and children and men were together again. Now we could surround our tormentors and fall upon them, one by one.

"The commander with three of his men succeeded in shooting, stabbing, thrusting his way back to the stair and the entrance. From there he tried by a signal whistle to gather his men back through the darkness. But not all were able to follow his signal.

"Meanwhile the young man, whose voice had bidden us put out the candles, had managed to get hold of a rifle. But we did not observe this until the S.S. men on the stair threw a searchlight upon us. Two quick shots destroyed the searchlight. Again we were under the cover of darkness. The same voice commanded us to disarm the S.S. men in our midst but to do them no hurt.

"It was only now that we recognized the voice. It was that of a simple villager, named Michael, but commonly called: Mechzio—the Penitent. He had arrived in our town a few weeks ago in order to pass the High Holidays with us. He earned his bread by assisting the beadle.

He was shy and taciturn. In his free hours he sat in the vestibule of the synagogue, where the smallest children learned their lessons. The children loved him because he was so big and strong and played all their games with them. They would tell us that the villager hardly knew how to pray. But they revered him because of his deep piety. It was the children, too, who had given him the name of Mechzio the Penitent.

"Had we in that dark hour been able to think or to wonder, we would probably have asked: how does it happen that this simple villager, Mechzio the Penitent—that he and none other has been sent us as a helper? But there was no time to ask or even to wonder. From the moment in which we had seen the bayoneted child we knew that our lives had become as cheap as the dust of the earth. He who helped us to sell our lives to our tormentors not quite for nothing, he was our true redeemer.

"But Mechzio the Penitent was intrepid enough to think differently. After he had shot the searchlight to pieces, he groped his way to that corner of the Hall of Prayer where there was the opening to the subterranean passage. He lifted up the stones and spoke again: 'Flee! Run to the cemetery! Run into the woods! There are only wild beasts in the woods.'

"Had we heard in time his warning to inflict no hurt upon the disarmed S.S. men, hundreds of us would perhaps have been saved in the forests. But the warning came too late. Nor had many understood why the murderers should not be hurt. Since the S.S. men were unable to rig up a second searchlight at once they tried to illuminate the place with their pocket flashlights. They cried out the names of the men who had remained in our midst. But since none of those who were called answered, they opened so murderous a fire upon the people in the darkness and continued that firing so long that nothing was heard in the Hall of Prayer but the silence of death.

"Thus not more than two and seventy souls escaped by way of the subterranean passage; women and children and men, mostly younger women and men and also, by Mechzio's assistance, the Torah scribe, his wife, his son Nehemiah and the girl Esther, the baker's daughter.

"On the next day the S.S. drove whatever Jews were left alive in the city to a playground. There again they divided them into two groups. They took one group out to the municipal forest. There many thousands of women and children and old men met the same fate which had overtaken the village Jews on Yom Kippur. The second group, consisting only of younger men and women, they escorted in several divisions to the houses of prayer and forced them to cleanse all these scenes of their crimes of the 'figures.' For living Jews the Germans had invented innumerable filthy appellations in their own tongue; their murdered victims they called by one word: 'figures.'

"It took some time before all the dead were huddled into a mass grave and all traces of blood obliterated. And from day to day the number of the grave diggers diminished, even as the number of the murdered victims increased. And when only those men and women and children were left who had been mustered out for forced labor in labor camps or for a special torture, the S.S. plundered the houses of their victims and set fire to the entire Jewish quarter.

"They let the old synagogue stand. Here they held captive fifty young girls, whom they had mustered out for a special function. After the city, in the parlance of the assassins, had been cleansed of Jews, they forced these girls to furnish and adorn the Hall of Prayer with the gear from the best houses of the city. The installation and decoration was guided by that same art rogue who had painted those shameful murals. As a covering for the stones of the floor the Torah scrolls seemed appropriate to this artist. Thereupon they opened the old synagogue as a house of lust for the front line officers. They called this brothel the temple on the Seret; they called these girls, the pious children of pious parents: priestesses of the temple.

"But these goings on were not destined to last. In

the third week after the opening of this place of traffic in lust, sundry higher officers came to visit the place. Among these was a man of the Catholic religion, who took umbrage at those images of the crucified. And he commanded them instantly to be obliterated. According to the evidence of the publican Andrej, the pictures were scrubbed out on three different occasions. And thrice they reappeared clearly in the sight of all. Thereupon the officers desisted from their amusement and fled from that place.

"The desecrated synagogue no longer seemed so homelike to the S.S. men either and they evacuated the brothel. They did that in their own manner; they set all the gear and adornments on fire. Then they took the tortured girls—whatever of them still remained—out to the municipal forest.

"Of the men and women who had saved their lives through the subterranean passage, the younger ones, led by Mechzio, fled into the forests where later they joined the forest fighters and, under the name of Partisans, acquired lasting fame. The old people and the children hid themselves in the clay caverns which formed the subterranean passage. Although they were furnished with food and water by Andrej and by the kindly sexton of the graveyard, occasionally too by Mechzio and his fellow fighters, only a few of them have survived in order to bear witness before this court.

"Of the children there have survived only Nehemiah, the son of the Torah scribe, and Esther, the baker's daughter. Sheva, too, is still alive. The aged Reb Zacharia Hakohen was still alive today. When Andrej's good message reached him, he pronounced a short prayer. Then he took his stick and said: 'My first errand in the open must be to see that good guardian of the cemetery who risked his own life in order to furnish us with water to drink.' Led by his wife he set out on his way to the cemetery. But at the exit of the passage he was surrounded by five soldiers whom that officer had sent down into the passage.

97

And one of them throttled the venerable man to death. Andrej, bring forth that murderer!"

As though he had been awaiting this summons, Andrej arose, revolver in hand, driving before him an S.S. man, whose hands had been tied with a rope. "The Reds have seized the other four. This is the murderer." "You were ordered to spy out the subterranean passage. That was all!" the officer yelled at him in blind rage. "I did it out of pity," said the S.S. man. "When we found him and told him he was the last Jew in the country, he said, 'If that's true I'd rather be dead too.' 'If you want to be dead,' I said to him, 'why don't you hang yourself?' 'Because I want you to take the blood guiltiness upon yourself,' said he. At that I grabbed him by the collar—and he was gone." "Stupid fool!" the officer cried. "We are behind the front now. We'll be prisoners soon!"

Now the Messenger interposed and said: "This crime is not adjudicable by this court. Our proceedings must be interrupted no more. For a danger is drawing near, a very great danger." "I know," said the accusing judge: "This crime does not belong here. What I wanted to make clear was this: that, even when they are beaten to the very earth, their minds do not turn to remorse and expiation but to murder and assassination. No *Ab-Beth-Din* would consider that an interruption of the proceedings."

"There also survives one of the forty-two scrolls of the Torah, the oldest of them all, which had been preserved in a special receptacle and had not been discovered by the blasphemers. Mechzio rescued it by night before the establishment of the brothel and the act of desecration. Today that scroll saved the life of the youth Nehemiah. He together with that Torah scroll will appear here at the proper moment. Otherwise he would have gone the way of his father.

"For a while all the survivors believed that the S.S. men had raged with special cruelty in this town. Be it declared in the sight of Heaven that this is not so. It is known to all the world how they sowed blood and death in all lands and in all cities, of which they made themselves the masters by the power of their armor. In this city, however, it came to pass that a child of thirteen confronted these evil ones. It happened here in this old synagogue. And for that reason this building became worthy of being the scene of this court. For here is the place of origin of the story of the S.S. man whose face was burned and of that other story of the images which refused to be obliterated."

"And these two stories blended into a single legend. And this legend of the Signs and Wonders beside the River Seret went from mouth to mouth, from village to village, from city to city, from land to land. And although the evil-doers cast forth their lying nets to snare this legend and, as though it were a Jewish child, to throttle it, they could not keep it from leaping across the boundaries of their own blood-guilty land.

"Here they sought to minimize the legend and to give it the form of a little story. In this form it came to the ears of one of the most powerful rulers of the realm, the Marshal, to him whom they called Fat-Belly. It was among the fat man's pleasures to amuse the Leader of the realm, whom they called the Screamer, with anecdotes. This happened during a session of the highest triumvirate of murder, to which belonged also that chief weaver of lies, whom they called the Club-Foot. The latter was much pleased by the anecdote. But the Screamer, who was incapable of laughter, grew somber of countenance and screamed: 'I will not have Jewish stories or miracles spread abroad even in jest. These stories are forbidden. They are forbidden even to the Marshal of the realm!'

"The Marshal, who was quite a warrior, would not for anything in the world have shown fear of the Leader

100

in the presence of the hated weaver of lies. He changed his tone and said: 'My purpose was very serious. It was I who warned against the public proclaiming of the extermination of the Jews and against carrying it out so coarsely in the light of history.'

" 'You warned against it?' cried the Screamer. 'Certainly, I warned against it. And once more I sound a warning in the name of our Master and Teacher who said: "Nothing better can be done for a faith than to set all the bloodhounds of the world upon its trail." It was thus that many teachings in the course of history have grown famous and mighty. We hunt the Jews and destroy their bodies. But we strengthen their faith. It is not hard to kill a million Jews. But try to execute a faith with machine guns or to throttle it with poison gas, and you will see whether our Teacher was right or not.'

" 'It goes without saying that he was right,' said the Screamer. 'But he lived in a time of degeneration and weakness and himself had not, despite his great wisdom, the strength to think his thoughts through to the very end. The greater disciple of our great Teacher has done so in his stead. It is I who say to you: if I exterminate the bearers of a faith to the last individual, I can exterminate it too. And that is true, above all, for Jews and Judaism. Indeed, it is wholly true in this case only. For that people and its faith are one.'

" 'Assuredly,' said Fat-Belly, 'you are the greater successor of our great teacher. But how will you accomplish that end? In Europe alone there are nine million Jews. Are you minded to destroy nine millions?' 'Why not?' said the Screamer. 'But since the Jews are a fertile people, there must be at least two million children among the nine millions,' said Fat-Belly. 'And will you destroy two million children?' 'Jew children? Why not? First and foremost the children.' The Screamer arose and, as was his custom, plunged into a convulsive ranting. 'Precisely, the children. Thus we cut off their future. Their present has been destroyed anyhow. The children, above all! Then we will put an end to their Heines and the Mendelssohns, the Mahlers, the Ehrlichs, the Schoenbergs, the Bergsons, and the Einsteins.

" 'I will instruct my Gestapo and my S.S. to make a thorough job of it. Where you find a Jew boy whose hands master the fiddle, first break his hands and next crush his skull. We don't need Offenbachs who enchant the Old World with their Jewish tricks nor Gershwins who enchant the New. Clean up! Be thorough, after our German fashion. It is highest time to cleanse the world.'

"And just as, according to a sudden impulse, he had plunged into ranting, so now he switched himself into a state of tranquillity, sat down again and, with a cold madness in his eyes, awaited the applause of his fellows. 'So be it! Magnificent, manly, German!' the weaver of lies interpolated and, while he expressed his enthusiasm, looked not at the admired Screamer but at the hated Fat-Belly.

" 'Magnificent. No doubt. As always,' said Fat-Belly. 'But what will the world and what will Rome say to this Pharaonic slaughter of the children?' 'It is I who can tell you that,' Club-Foot hastened to answer. 'When we announced to the world that we would let escape any Jew whom that world would provide for in its sparsely inhabited colonial areas, all the lands of the world slammed their gates. Here and there they opened them a little in order to admit a Jew who would be useful or profitable to them. Such is the answer of the world which in its hypocrisy preaches humanity to us. What Rome will say, I will ask our Leader to foretell prophetically.' "

" 'There are two Romes,' the Screamer said quietly. 'You mean the political Rome? It will keep its mouth shut and will continue to serve my purposes. As far as the spiritual Rome is concerned, I have instructed my ambassador to sound it out and to give me a report on Rome's attitude toward our solution of the Jewish problem. The report is brief: Rome is discreet.' There was resounding laughter.

" 'How handsome of them,' said Fat-Belly. 'Rome is discreet. And will remain so, I suspect. So that question is settled. Now let us come back to the beginning of our consultation. I don't doubt that we will succeed in cleansing Europe of Jews. And you know me well enough to know that I shan't regret it. However, if a job like that is done, we must expect it to cry to Heaven. And when a thing like that happens—' 'You think Heaven may answer?' the Leader interrupted him and Club-Foot screamed with laughter again.

" 'Heaven, of course, will not answer,' said Fat-Belly. 'But in such cases there are always those who believe that they hear an answer from Heaven. Thus legends arise. Our own people are hardly composed of those who expect Heaven to speak. Yet among us there are millions who believe that the sun will shine through rain and storm, whenever our Leader mounts the speaker's tribune.'

" 'But in that case it it true,' said Club-Foot and looked up piously at the Screamer who, on his part, measured Fat-Belly with a murderous glance. 'So you see, my Leader,' said the Marshal of the realm, 'he, too, believes in miracles, even in the miracles which he himself invents. Now the Jews, whatever else they may be, surpass even our miracle maker here in their belief in the supernatural. I see a real danger in this circumstance. And I would like to have warned against it. We have not yet conquered the world.'

" 'Victory or not! After me no Burim will be celebrated,' cried the Screamer who was about to plunge into another ranting convulsion, but he stopped himself and merely repeated: 'After me, no Burim will be celebrated because there will be no Jews left to do so!' The Screamer meant to say Purim. But since his nose was stopped up, quite like his brain and heart, he said Burim.

" 'True, after us Purim must cease,' Club-Foot agreed. 'And I imagine that I have found a sure way of robbing the surviving Jews of their low delight in surviving, once and for all. We're not the first men in history who set themselves the aim of exterminating the Jews. But hitherto all such attempts have failed. Why? Because all

103

our predecessors committed the same error, that, namely, of making the Jew a tragic figure in history. In the Middle Ages the Church built thousands of pyres for the Jews and roasted them by the thousands. Yet they survived the fires. Why? Because the Church said to the Jews: "Give up your faith or your life." The Jew gave up his life and thus perished as a tragic hero. From a thousand deaths he arose in a thousand resurrections.

" 'We've avoided this error. We have given the Jews no choice. We say: first your money, then your life. Since they have no choice, they have no tragic character. So it was a wise idea of our Leader to make no secret of the extermination of the Jews. We kill them in the broad light of history. And we proclaim it to all the world. Thus we cause the extermination to be regarded as a lawful process. So far, so good. But only so far. For it is not to be denied that the Marshal's warning is not wholly wrong. For we must not forget that if we now turn this war of extermination against the children, the situation will become more favorable to the Jews. For in the case of children, the question of choice does not arise. Children are always martyrs. Now every martyrdom is illustrious. How much more the martyrdom of children! A way must therefore be found to extinguish the lives of these children and the glory of their martyrdom at the same time.'

" 'From what I know of you, you would not mention the means toward such an end, if you had not already thought of it,' said Fat-Belly. 'So let's hear what it is.'

"Club-Foot decided to transform this challenge into an acknowledgment of his efficiency. He said: 'Certainly, I have always preferred the precision of action to the vagueness of speech. I have indeed found a means which we must now begin to use. We have succeeded up to now in rendering life so unbearable to the Jews that they have herded themselves like sheep to the slaughter or have even taken their own lives. If ever, as in that dark synagogue, they undertake something resembling resistance, they do it after the manner of a rat which cannot extricate its teeth from the stick that slays it. In brief: we have done a brilliant job with living Jews. But how about the dead Jews, the *Figures*? We throw them into mass graves or we burn them in crematories. Similar things have happened among the best peoples. For the people of Israel we must invent something new. We have made a shameful thing of their lives; we must desecrate their death. That is a cynical notion and when you have a cynical notion, the best thing to do with it is to submit it to the scientists. It is surprising how many clever answers our professors had, when this problem was brought before them. Professor Johann Sebastian Knecht of Tuebingen, for instance, estimated for me that the amount of phosphorus in a Figure would suffice to produce two thousand matches. Not a bad idea. But too expensive. Another professor explained to me that the human body contains such other chemical substances, as calcium, sugar, copper, iron. Nonsense? Certainly. But out of the nonsense of the professors I picked one excellent idea. To put it briefly: you can make something out of the fat of the Figures. What? Something which will, in the truest sense of the adverb, cleanly solve the problem. What is this thing? Soap. This soap will render the atmosphere of Jewish martyrdom quite pure. Wherever a piece of that soap falls, the soil will grow no legends. And so their very death will become a shameful thing.'

" 'And are we going to cry this out to all the world, too?' Fat-Belly asked the Screamer. In his stead Club-Foot answered: 'God forbid, no! We will have it whispered from mouth to mouth and deny it publicly. And I will weave it so subtly and spin it out so fine, that the world will both believe and disbelieve, that it will know everything and pretend to know nothing. Not even the Jews will know what is being done to them. And the Jews in foreign lands will be silenced by very shame. A Jew may loudly lament over the fact that his brother, his son, his father has been killed by poison gas. He will not want to boast that his grandmother has been turned into soap.'

105

"The Marshal sat still with lowered lids. The enormous opulence of his body oozed beyond the framework of his upholstered chair. From his womanish breasts the numerous medals and decorations hung down over the taut curvature of his belly like a rain-soaked flag over the mounded grave of a hero. He was a hell of a fellow, this Marshal of the realm. Far superior in active evil to the malicious, simian weaver of lies. But the determination to make soap of human flesh affected him like a thrust in the belly. He had to control himself with all his might not to show a sign of nausea. But he did control himself and said: 'Abominable as this means may be, it may also be effective. The chief devil of hell could not think up anything more devilish. But I am bound to ask one thing: you are both the sons of Christian Catholic parents. Neither one of you has gotten himself to the point of seceding from the Church. You know better than I the teaching of the Church concerning the reappearance of the Redeemer at the end of time. Will he not again be of the seed of David? Is it not possible that the Redeemer will be born again somewhere as a Jewish child? Will you take it upon yourself to make soap of the body of the Redeemer? We hoped to rank you in universal history with Alexander the Great and Napoleon Bonaparte. Do you prefer to stand by the side of Pharaoh and Herod?'

"The Screamer relished such questions above all else. In token of the circumstance that he was speaking in the character of a world historic person, he arose and said: 'I have not seceded from the Church, because I have always avoided giving a warning to powerful enemies. The Church is still a powerful enemy. But once the Jews are exterminated, the very root will be gone and the whole of Christianity will drop like a rotten tooth out of the pus-filled jaw of Europe. I secede from the Church? I will force the Church to secede from Europe! History asks no questions. But were it ever to ask the question, what is more precious to me: to conquer the world or to turn the Figure of the Jewish Redeemer into soap, my answer is in readiness. After me there will be neither Burim nor Christmas, neither Paschal Feasts nor Good Friday!'

"And he commanded Club-Foot to inaugurate the warfare against Jewish children. And he gave him a free hand to proceed with the Figures as his judgment bade him do."

"The searching out of evil is the duty of the narrating judge. But perhaps too crass a description will have to be expunged from the records of this court," said the *Ab Beth-Din.* And at his beckoning the accusing judge spoke once again:

"Hitherto the defilers of Creation had done their bloody work without respect of age or sex. Now their madness wreaked itself upon the tenderest and the weakest. In their own land as well as in the twenty lands which they had overrun with their armored cars, there began a dreadful hunting of Jewish children and pregnant women. And the bloody hand of the hunter and of the beater was upon all cities, all villages, all houses, all hiding places, where the hunted and the hounded dwelt or sought concealment. For in all the twenty lands they found accomplices, whether hired murderers or degenerate madmen.

"And along the boundaries of those larger or smaller countries, which had not yet fallen into the sombre realms of German victory, they placed armed frontier guards. These guards had sharp eyes; they did not sleep by night, as did not the hunters and the beaters. And if it happened that one of the hounded mothers—one among ten thousand—succeeded in reaching a frontier with a child, the guards stopped her and asked her: 'Have you a passport?'

And if the mother did have a passport, they asked: 'Have you a visa, too? And have you money? Are you a Jewess? And is your child a Jewish child?' And they would drive mother and child back into the toils of the hunters and into destruction.

"In this period the Germans had already erected their factories of death. There were the great ones: Auschwitz, Maidanek, Treblinka; there were smaller ones. In all of these the murder of a people was accomplished in true German fashion, methodically and scientifically. And in all the twenty countries which they had overrun there were innumerable gathering places in innumerable cities where the victims of their lust for murder were assembled in order to be transported to the slaughtering houses.

"And they counted the victims and branded their skin with symbols and numbers, in order that any who escaped might be recognized as a victim of the slaughterer and not escape the knife.

"And they emptied the school houses and the orphan houses and the kindergartens and loaded the children on trucks and cattle cars. And they treated these children with a cruelty which not the most inhuman slaughterer of beasts was wont to use. For has one ever heard of a slaughterer who sends sheep to a distant slaughter house without providing them with feed and water on the way? Or whoever heard of a butcher so brutal that with iron-shod boots he trod upon the calves in a wagon, as though they were bundles of straw, in order that the wagon might hold more calves than its space permitted?

"We have the evidence of sworn witnesses who beheld with their own eyes S.S. men and Gestapo men committing crimes of this kind. For unlike other slaughterers, these German warriors were not interested in having their victims live until they reached the slaughter house.

"For three years the freight trains with their freight of children rolled through the twenty lands of the civilized world. By day men saw them roll and went to their work.

109

By night women heard them, while they sang lullabies to their own children.

"And upon the whole of this continent there was to be found no power, either secular or spiritual, which was willing to raise either an arm or a cry and bid these trains to cease rolling.

"And all these trains reached their destination. And at every such destination there stood a factory of death. And their gates opened to receive the freight of children. And the children who were still alive had to help carry the children who were already dead into the death factories, in order to conform to the bills of lading: Freight On Board: One thousand children. Received seven hundred and seventy-six alive, two hundred and twenty-four as Figures. And this had to be so. Because wherever the German rules, order must prevail.

"Only the chief murderers know exactly how many children were slaughtered. We are dependent on estimates. But according to all human judgment our estimates are exact, grievously exact, exact with the silence of death. They cut off one third of the body and the life of our people, namely, six millions. They have cut out one third of our very heart: eleven hundred thousand children; eleven hundred thousand.

"We counted them in twenty lands, in hundreds of cities, in thousands of houses. We counted them in the schools and in the orphan houses and in the nursery schools. Everywhere, where once there was laughter and childish tears and joy and play and the singsong of study and the confusion of childish delight, everywhere there was silence.

"And in this deathly silence we counted our dead children. We counted them from land to land, from city to city, from village to village. And with the number of the dead there grew and grew the torment of the counters of the dead. We, the orphans, the survivors, we have become a people of the counters of the dead. Twelve million who count the dead, and six million dead and among them eleven hundred thousand children.

"Among these children were some who were Jewish children only according to the German law concerning the blood. These children did not know why they had to die, and in the hands of the hangmen they cried out after their mothers. But among them were also pious children, little disciples of the Torah with sidecurls and believing eyes under their luminous foreheads. These children knew why they were hounded and tortured and slain. When the hand of the hangman was upon them, they cried not after their mother; they cried after their Father, their Father in Heaven, and with the dying declaration of their faith they perished for the Sanctification of the Name.

"And even as the murderers did not discriminate between those children and these, so we do not discriminate and we say: Those children and these children are all our children and they all died for the Sanctification of the Name Who will avenge the blood of the martyrs.

"And even as the murderers did not discriminate among these children in the matter of torture and death, even so the defilers made no discrimination in the matter of defilement. As it had been decided in the council of the three chief murderers, so defilement everywhere followed upon slaughter. They caused the hair of the dead to be sheared and sent the hair of the children to workshops to make mattresses of them. They sent the Figures to workshops where cleansing material was manufactured. There the flesh, taken from the bones, was boiled and turned into that substance which the weaver of lies had thought out as a cure against legends.

"And they called this substance Figure Soap, or even Genuine Figure Soap or, at times, Warranted Genuine Figure Soap. And they packed up this product in boxes and sent the boxes out wherever their Gestapo and their S.S. men held power, especially the power of spreading rumors and of mixing lies with truth in such a manner, that no one

111

was able to determine what was to be believed and what not.

"The first box they sent out in honor of him whose face had been burned to a crisp, namely, to S.S. Number 27. This echelon which, like the entire German army, had first stumbled from victory to victory, now, after the battle of Stalingrad, like the entire German army, fled from defeat to defeat and changed their station from week to week. The box, however, did not drift about to find the Echelon 27. It was sent on the right road and arrived at the right place at the right time. Here it is now, at the place of judgment."

The accuser arose from his seat and gave a signal to the soldier whose forehead was bandaged and said to him: "Go over there and read us the inscription on the cover of the box. Read it out aloud. And you, Reb Senderl, go and open the box and bring whatever you find in it to the table of the judges."

THE NINETEENTH CHAPTER

The bandaged man arose from the steps. With rapid tread he went to the box which had been placed under the smaller image of the crucified and, as he had been ordered, read out in a loud voice and in soldierly obedience the inscription on the box:

WARRANTED GENUINE FIGURE SOAP
FOR THE HEROES OF S.S. 27
WITH THE GRATITUDE OF THE LEADER. CHRISTMAS, 1943

Reb Senderl, the water carrier, meanwhile remembered how three pairs of publicans' hands, as practiced as they were skillful, had sought to open the box in vain. And so he approached it with hesitating steps. Scarcely had the soldier completed the reading, than Reb Senderl with three crooked fingers grasped a corner of what seemed to be the cover of the box. And he turned an expression of childlike wonder at the publican Andrej, when he became aware that the cover of the box, under the pressure of his fingers, began to move in its grooves and glided noiselessly to the floor.

And so it was Reb Senderl alone, among those present, who did not become immediately aware of what was hidden in the box. Terror struck upon them all. Those who were still sitting leaped up. Those who were standing recoiled violently. Even the six judges arose from their chairs, and it was apparent that even they had not been prepared for this sight. When they saw the Figure in the box their eyes grew rigid and their beards trembled.

In the box stood the Figure of a boy of thirteen. With its yellow, waxen skin, it seemed a plastic replica of that smaller image of the crucified one beneath which it stood within the framework of the gleaming wood of the box, at once ghostly and yet corporeally real, in the exact dimension of life. And as the twilight in the old synagogue blended with the twilight in the box, even so the image on the wall blended with the statue in the box in such a manner, that the water carrier who was the last to perceive it, was the first to recognize it and to give it a name: "Jochanan! That is Jochanan, the son of the Torah scribe."

The water carrier remembered now, how, many years ago, he had saved the twins from the river. And so he took no fright at the rigidity and silence of the boy. He needed no monition from the accusing judge to lift the body from its wood frame. He lifted it with careful and tender hands, even as a pious man lifts the Torah scroll out of the Ark. And even as a pious man honors the Torah scroll with a pressure of his lips, the while he lets it glide into the crook of his left arm and presses it to his bosom, even thus Reb Senderl kissed that pale boyish forehead before he pressed the body with both arms against his breast. Then he bore it swiftly to the judges' table on the Almemor.

With frightened face the wounded soldier followed Reb Senderl who, with groping feet, mounted the steps to the Almemor. There the soldier drew himself up to his full height and addressed the judges with raised voice: "Honorable court! I am not one of these S.S. murderers. I am a soldier. I was wounded this morning. These S.S. men found me hurt amid the ruins of a house and took me with them. But, as God is my witness, I am not one of them."

On the Almemor the *Ab Beth-Din* went to meet the sobbing water carrier by three paces. He received from him the boyish body and laid it gently on the judges' table. Then he said to the wounded soldier: "What you say is known to this court. Fear not! You have been called here to bear witness." While the soldier bowed deep before the judges, the *Ab Beth-Din* urged haste once more: "The accuser! The accuser!"

All the judges resumed their seats. But the accusing judge, with lowered head and lowered lids, stood for a while as though he had lost the power of speech. Then, not turning his eyes from the boyish body before him, he said: "In the face of what we see here accusation itself fades and falls silent."

"The defender! Where is the defender?" asked the *Ab Beth-Din*. "Where there is no accuser, there can be no court; where there is no defender, there can be no sentence," the expert declared. "Hence the proceedings should be put off." "Will you undertake the defense?" the *Ab Beth-Din* asked the priest. "No," said the priest, "I am here only in the capacity of an expert." "And I in that of an observer," the second priest hastened to add.

"A defender has announced his coming," said the *Ab Beth-Din*. "For the second time we summon him to appear. Whether he come in good or evil intent, we now summon him for the third time to appear." "Perhaps the defender was already here," said the accuser. "Perhaps at the sight of what we see his words perished upon his lips, too. Who could utter a word in the defense of the murderers of eleven hundred thousand children, unless it be Satan himself?"

"*Al tiftah peh lesatan!*" warned the *Ab Beth-Din*. "Call not upon Satan! He alone would try to disturb the procedure of this court. That shall not be. It shall not be interrupted. Thrice have we called the defender in vain, and since no one who is present feels called upon to undertake the defense, we will let the assumption of the accuser stand: Only Satan would presume to appear as a defender in this action."

And therewith the *Ab Beth-Din* took a sheet of paper

115

and he wrote down sundry questions and he read these questions at once to his fellow judges. The first question concerned guilt and said: Guilty or not guilty? The second question was a question concerning punishment and it said: Guilty and cast out. The third question was again a question concerning the nature of the punishment and it said: Guilty and forever rejected.

Thereupon he instructed the judges saying: "This court has not the power to execute a sentence. The sentence of this court is in the true sense of the word an act of cognition. Yet it will assume both power and validity, insofar as it corresponds to the sentence of the Court on High, which is simultaneously in session and awaits the sentence of this court."

Meanwhile there appeared on the steps near the entrance that stranger, whom the children of the Torah scribe had called "the Round One." And with his nasal voice he called out to the court: "*Audiatur et altera pars!*" The other party must have a hearing, too! And without awaiting an answer, he made his way through the group of the S.S. men, who had gathered in the course of the proceedings, and like a blown up ball he trundled down the stair, step by step.

When he arrived in front of the Messenger, he prolonged his leap through the air, so that his short legs missed a step and with an anxious glance at the Messenger, who tried, as it were, to wave the intruder aside, he repeated his cry: "*Audiatur et altera pars!*"

"And who are you?" the young priest addressed him, perhaps because he used Latin. "I have been sent here, to use your language, as the *advocatus diaboli*, the devil's advocate," the Round One answered the priest, without interrupting his hopping. When he had arrived at the foot of the Almemor he stood still; he bowed as much as his figure would permit him; he said in a soft voice: "I come from the *sitra ahra*."

"And so the *sitra ahra*, the other, under side, is taking a hand," said the *Ab Beth-Din* to the accusing judge.

"Light the black candles." While the youngest of the judges took seven black candles from the drawer of the judges' table, lit them with trembling hands and gave one to each of the seven judges, the Round One hopped up the steps of the Almemor. But when he beheld the black candles he stopped short on the top step and said in a hurt voice: "This defense is not needed. Although I come from the *sitra ahra*, I do not come in evil intent."

"If you come as a defender, you come belatedly but not quite unexpectedly. But you are to know that these judges cannot be confused," said the *Ab Beth-Din*. "I'm surprised that we were expected," said the Round One. "I'm very much surprised. To be sure, we had encouraged someone to take up the defense, but it was not one of us. A legal scholar of world repute had volunteered his services."

"We have called upon him thrice," said the accusing judge, "but he did not put in an appearance. Why?" "The dear good man," answered the Round One, "started out in ample time. But not far from here he fell into the hands of the Germans. Since he looked like a scholar and had no identity papers, they took him to be a Jew and killed him. It would be funny if it weren't so tragic. My Master was willing to call it a day. He took no interest in the defense of the murderers of children. He was simply eager to find out what a legal light of such reputation would be able to think out as a defense of these murderers. Now since the murderers themselves destroyed their defender, my Master decided to take no part in this proceeding. Only at the last moment, literally the very last, as you see, was I sent here.

"Why? Well, that has to do with your formulation in the matter of punishment, actually with the formulation of a single question, namely, guilty and cast out. My Master is not at all pleased with this formulation. It irritates him, hurts him, challenges him. What did you mean by that? Does not this court know that, among other names, my Master also bears the name of him who is cast out but not rejected forever?

"On the one hand this court says: *al tiftah peh lesatan*. On the other hand, it formulates a question in such a manner as to be a direct challenge to my Master. 'Run,' my Master said to me. 'Run as fast as you can and speak an open word.' You see I'm quite breathless and my forehead is perspiring." And the Round One raised the back of his hand to wipe his forehead, a gesture which he had used from his very appearance on with almost theatrical exaggeration.

"If your Master considers the matter of this court so important and if you, indeed, appear in no evil intention, tell us why you assume this blown up corpulence, which would seem to contradict both the haste and the import of your errand?" asked the *Ab Beth-Din*. And all the judges looked with astonishment, even with consternation, upon the presiding judge as though he had permitted himself an inappropriate jest.

"That has been arranged in order to remain within the right similitude," the round man replied with a smile which did not again recede from his buttery fat face: "A good deal of nonsense is taught and believed about us everywhere. But the saying that the sins of mankind make Satan fat is full of good sense. Since that somber hound, whom the Germans chose as their messiah, has become so active, we have all grown so fat that we can hardly move. All this, naturally, only within the similitude. You call me corpulent? You should see my Master! For long now we call His Excellency no other than His Opulency. Naturally, only in jest, after the manner of a similitude.

"I perceive, *Ab Beth-Din*, that this court is properly conducted. Your question was a wise one and very acceptable to us. I speak openly, as I was commanded to do, and I say: Yes, Satan has enough. You know how that is to be interpreted. The boldest interpretation would not yet be bold enough. Does that suffice you? I have no authority to go beyond that. You observe that the Messenger over there gave you no clear hint either.

"All this I say in the name of my Master whose

voice, as it were, I am. I am his pupil, too, and as such may be permitted to add: The Germans have succeeded in making evil so revolting that even Satan is nauseated. They are fond of the measureless. In a short time they have amassed evil so monstrously that it stinks not only to heaven but even more to hell. This, too, of course, is metaphorical. But we hold our noses not only over the monstrous quantity of evil. It is also from the kind practiced by the Germans that Satan averts his once angelic face. The Germans have applied the dull coarseness of the slaughter house to the murder of man. They consider it daemonic to make soap of human flesh, yet this is but the manner of stupid butchers, of industrious meat cutters, of blood-sprent seethers of soap. *De gustibus non est disputandum*—but there exists, after all, good taste and bad. And what the Germans call devilish, the devil calls German.

"And here I am impelled once more to praise the wisdom of this court. It is as deep and clear as a pure spring. The longer one gazes into it, the more clearly does one see the bottom. I confess that it annoyed me that the accuser was forbidden properly to delineate before this court the mad and bloody deeds committed against children. I now see that I was foolishly mistaken. It would be a shame to clothe such shame in word, in color or in sound. It would be shameless to lay bare such shame even before the judges in a court.

"In order to delineate what these defilers of Creation have done, one would have to be of their kind. And it is to be feared that this oaf, once the weapons have been snatched from his hand, will once again sentimentally drag himself to the side of his German soulfulness and break out in an infinitely melodious belching and declare that belching to be a *Nibelungenlied*.

"Nevertheless, it seems appropriate to me to interpose a single objection: a further limitation should be put upon the wise restraint of the court. The accusation gives a number: eleven hundred thousand children were slaugh-

119

tered. A round number. But numbers and figures have neither countenance, nor heart, nor eyes. But the eleven hundred thousand children had eleven hundred thousand faces; they had eleven hundred thousand hearts; they had twice eleven hundred thousand eyes. How much light has been exinguished! In twice eleven hundred thousand extinguished children's eyes there is space for a darkness great enough to hide this entire continent in an eternal night.

"Perhaps it will be asked: How does it become you, Messenger of Satan, how does it become you to use such language? In this part of the earth my Master has been most blasphemously traduced. On the one hand he is known as the poor old devil, who frightens peasants and women and children, the ensnarer of souls and of rats. On the other hand, he is represented as a great lord, a sovereign and sombre prince of hell, the rival and adversary of the 'dear, good God' in Heaven. It cannot be unknown to this court that once upon a time my Master had six pairs of wings and bore the title: *Malakh shel rahamim*, the angel of compassion. How would it be if it occurred to my Master to reiterate today at the highest bar of judgment his irreversible claim to this beautiful title? This court knows the difference between being thrust out and being rejected. Expunge this question, which is an error here, out of the book of this court! Extinguish the black candles! Satan's abhorrence of these slaughterers of children, Satan's pity for your children, is not to be misinterpreted. Before this figure Satan stands, as we all do, in tears." And as he had again and again dried the sweat of his forehead with his hand, so, while he was speaking, the Round One raised both of his hands to dry his eyes as he fell silent.

THE TWENTIETH CHAPTER

Hereupon the *Ab Beth-Din* spoke once more: "The wisdom of this court, which you have so extravagantly praised, is small, much smaller than its determination to render justice in a world without justice, a world which is tempted to hide or even adorn its blasphemous indifference with a false and hypocritical compassion.

"This world without justice is already preparing to forget what has been done to us and to itself. From lying throats the cry is already heard—the cry for compassion. Compassion for whom? For the victims? No! For the hangmen. But we, we say: Let judgment prevail! For it is written: *Kol derakhav mishpat,* Judgment is upon all His ways. Pass judgment, for we will be judged. Judge, else the law withers and becomes chaff before the wind. Let the judges be mindful of the martyr Rabbi Chanina ben Tradion, who did not forgive his Roman tormentors but went to his fiery death with a cry after retaliation.

"Before, however, the judges reach their final sentence, let us justify ourselves once more. I am in dread in the matter of the wisdom of this court. Its poor wisdom has been praised too highly, far too highly, perhaps in order to confuse us.

"Above three years we lived in graves and in dark caverns. Have we lived to see the light of day because we,

121

all older men, were so very wise? Many miracles have happened to us. But the greatest wonder, the perpetual wonder, which preserved us in life when we were so near to death, was it not a child, a boy, now a youth, by the name of Nehemiah? Who brought us bread, when the gifts of the good publican Andrej failed to reach us? Who spoke consoling words to us when despair overcame us? Who thrice a day added to each prayer his own prayer: 'Amalek will not overcome us; Amalek will be put to shame and it is we who will live.' A thousand times he was near death, this son of a Torah scribe, and a thousand times he raised us up by his faith, his strength, his confidence. Now we sit here, all of us older men, and we are to sit in judgment upon the crimes committed against our children. And shall it be that our dearest one, Nehemiah, is not to be heard? Delay was danger but just now haste is our present danger. Where is Nehemiah? His mother is here, Esther is here, all those who were saved are here. Why does Nehemiah linger?"

The wife of the Torah scribe sat at one of the broken prayer desks. Her eyes, long unaccustomed to the light of day, were closed. Her head leaned gently against the shoulder of the girl Esther. Whether it was that the old woman, petrified by her grief, was not accessible to questioning, or whether it was that her hearing had been impaired, she was not aware of the question and did not stir from her rigidity.

In her stead the girl Esther made reply: "Nehemiah has gone to the old cemetery in order to bring forth from its hiding place the rescued Torah scroll. Mechzio is with him. Without the Torah scroll Nehemiah is unwilling to appear here." "Esther, ask Sheva, the widow of the Torah scribe, whether she has the strength to give evidence before this court, before her son appears," the accusing judge said to the girl Esther.

At that the old woman began to stir and said: "Let my son Nehemiah bear witness; let him bear witness for me too. I, myself, would like to ask questions, many questions. For instance, why did it have to come to pass that there is no *minyan*, why there are no ten men, to say *Kaddish* for the Torah scribe? With Mechzio and with my son, there are but nine of you and you cannot provide a *minyan* to say *Kaddish* for the Torah scribe. Is it not so? Out of the darkness of the graves I rose to the light of day after so many years and I went into the city to look for the tenth man. There had been six and twenty thousand of our faith in this town. Now is that town a broken shard and there are not ten men to form a *minyan*. Is the Torah scribe to be borne to his grave without *Kaddish*?

"And furthermore I would ask: why is every prediction made to us only half fulfilled? Two sons were promised me; now I have but one and must consider myself doubly favored. For what Jewish mother has still even one son? It was foretold of us that we would be as numerous as the sands on the seashore and the stars in the sky. We have indeed become like the sand upon which any who desire may tread. But have we become like the stars in the sky? It has been foretold of us that, at the end of time, our life would become as hard as the task of one who must climb a wall of ice. Behold, O Judges, our life has become as hard as that of him who must climb a wall of ice. But is *this* the end of time? Behold, O Judges, I have the strength to ask; have you the strength to answer me?"

It was now that sharp rifle fire was heard in front of the synagogue. Immediately thereupon a troop of Red soldiers with raised weapons entered by the door. The S.S. men threw up their arms. Like a pack of dogs obedient to the whistle of a master of the hounds, they ran over the steps into captivity. The Reds let them approach one by one. They counted their captives after the manner of the Tatars by kicking each S.S. man out of doors with a heavy boot in his behind.

The S.S. heroes, so intrepid in their war against Jewish children and women and old men, accepted these kicks with a pale grin, as though the matter were a soldier's jest.

Still sitting on the stairs, the wife of the Torah scribe watched this incident with both consternation and satisfaction. She said to the girl Esther: "Go, my daughter, to those good foot-soldiers and ask them if perhaps in their midst there is a tenth man for our *minyan*?" When the girl hesitated, the old woman tried to lift herself to her feet. She desisted from this attempt when she heard the voice of her son, who now appeared in the company of the man Michael, called Mechzio.

Slowly those two come down the stair. Nehemiah saluted those present with a festive greeting: "Amalek has not prevailed; Amalek has been put to shame. Amalek lies in the dust." In his arms he held the rescued Torah scroll, clad in its covering of purple velvet, crowned with its silver crown. Mechzio had a pistol in his right hand. Both were clad in clay-stained peasant smocks; in honor of the day they were girded with narrow black girdles.

From the stair that leads to the Almemor Nehemiah looked about. He beheld the S.S. officer and the wounded soldier, both of whom the Reds had left to the court. He said: "You wage war against the children of Israel, against the teachings of Israel, against the Guardian of Israel. The Creator of the World and His teachings and His people are indivisible. Against this trinity none will prevail. You hunters of men are now the hunted. The powers which now hunt you, be they called what they will, whether in the East or in the West, are in this hour the outstretched arm, His arm, the arm of wrath against you."

Thereafter he turned again, looked up at the Almemor and raised his voice: "Has the court decided upon its judgment? If so, tell me, *Ab Beth-Din*, what is the final cognition of the court?" The judges, who had risen in honor of the rescued Torah, fixed their eyes upon the *Ab Beth-Din*, and their faces seemed as white as the white Yom Kippur shrouds, which they had donned again in

124

order to pronounce judgment. "While the victors counted their captives, this court, in order to refrain from interrupting its proceedings, decided not to await your evidence. For the court has already rendered an unanimous decision. The conclusion is one of compassion, of compassion for the victims. The judgment is: 'Guilty. Thrice guilty. Guilty and forever rejected.' And you, Nehemiah ben Zacharia, have been found worthy of pronouncing sentence."

The Round One, when he heard this decision, hopped around the circle of the judges in unrestrained delight. Then he cast a glance of jubilation at the place on the stair where the Messenger had been standing. But since he no longer saw the Messenger there, disappointment replaced delight upon his round face. With lightning speed, so that his hopping from place to place, from step to step, seemed transformed into flight, he disappeared. The Messenger, moreover, had become invisible at that moment when on the steps the prisoners began to be counted and on the Almemor the sentence of the court to be written down.

While Nehemiah, the Torah scroll in his arms, carefully mounted the steps leading to the Almemor, the judges extinguished the black candles, seeing that the Round One had disappeared. But they continued to form a circle about the table of judgment, in order not to expose Nehemiah suddenly and without preparation for that which lay upon it.

On the Almemor, Nehemiah handed the Torah to the *Ab Beth-Din* who embraced it, honored it with a kiss and then caused it similarly to be handed from judge to judge. Having gone through the circle of judges it returned to his own arms.

Nehemiah stood for a while without stirring. His face was turned to the east wall. He was almost seventeen now and grown quite tall. His form was delicate and his narrow, peaked face seemed composed only of the light of his forehead, the fire of his eyes and the redness of his mouth. He chanted a prayer with a voice so hushed and low that even the judges did not catch the words but only the melody of a Yom Kippur chant arising, as it were, out of a grave. His feet were close together, almost folded, and his body swayed to the right and to the left and again to the right and to the left and bowed and swayed again, even as a reed does in a wind.

THE TWENTY-FIRST CHAPTER

Suddenly, as though a monitory hand had touched his shoulder, he turned sideways. His eye was now upon the stair near the door, where the Messenger had become visible again, and in a loud melodious voice he began to read the sentence of the court:

"The defilers of creation, the Soilers of the Source— may their name be blotted out of the Book of Life and out of the Book of Death. May a burning fire and a searing bolt corrode and expunge from the face of humanity any and every lineament which may recall these Nazi-Germans, whether in body or in spirit.

"The blood which they have shed will rise up against them. Those whom they have hunted, whom they have humiliated, whom they have tortured, whom they have wounded with knives, whom they have burned with fire, whom they have drowned in water, whom they have throttled with poisonous gases; the flesh which they have torn, the bones which they have broken, the skin which they have lacerated, the blood which they have shed—all this will rise up against them and will throttle and choke them and obliterate them from the face of earth. The murderers of children and the burners of children, the doers and the instigators, the robbers and the receivers of what was robbed, the informers and the accomplices in

127

murder and in torture, may their name be blotted out of the Book of Life and out of the Book of Death. They will not escape this curse.

"No, they will in no wise escape this curse, nor will any of those escape punishment who in twenty lands were the idle witnesses of these monstrous deeds committed against our children, who were the children of their land, when the hand of the hangman was stretched out after these children. No, they will not escape punishment, even as those others will not escape it, who even now are willing to wash clean the still blood-sprent hand of the hangman, those sensitive souls who can less easily endure the sight of a hanged hangman than the sight of a suckling babe under an iron heel. No, they will in no wise avoid punishment and disgrace, those forgetters and forgivers, those men of gold and pelf, who are even now very busy shaking those bloody hands. That blood, which they have helped to shed, that blood which they would fain forget—it will rise up against them and thrust them into disgrace and shame.

"But even as we consign to the irrevocable curse of shame and of disgrace the defilers of creation and their henchmen, as well as the idle witnesses and the forgetters and forgivers—even so would we here commemorate with imperishable honor and an eternal blessing those human beings who, at the risk of their own lives, gave consolation to the disconsolate, refuge to the hunted, bread to the starving, water to the famishing. For even in the German Sodom and the German Gomorrha, as in sundry other lands, there were to be found such venerable men and women, worthy of our blessing, wherever the hunters of men hounded the children of Israel.

"Though their number, to the shame of all humanity, was but small, their memory will be sacredly guarded by us. A time will come in which we will enter their names into the Book of this court and read them to our children on the commemorative day of this martyrdom, which will be a day both of fasting and of feasting. For after the passing of that dark hound, there will be Purim again and a Paschal Feast, as well as Christmas and Good Friday until that end of time, which shall see the rising of a single and great Sabbath, as the sun of redemption for all, save only those who have been rejected in time and in eternity."

Nehemiah fell silent. He bowed his forehead and covered it with his hands. After a period of anxiety, for it seemed as though a weakness had overcome him, he lowered his hands from his forehead, looked straight into the face of the Messenger and said to him: "This, Messenger, is our message for you. Do you now tell us what message you have."

"Nehemiah ben Zacharia Hakohen," the Messenger said, "you have been found worthy of pronouncing the sentence of this court. You have been found worthy—on account of the merits of your father, Zacharia Hakohen, and on account of the merits of your younger brother, Jochanan ben Zacharia Hakohen—to pronounce judgment too, now, in the name of the Court on High. For that Court on High and this court have now become one and the same, since the Court Above by Its ruling has now validated the ruling of this earthly court."

Thereupon Nehemiah turned around and, spreading out his arms, approached the circle of the judges. The *Ab Beth-Din*, being of the opinion that the youth was spreading out his arms for the reception of the Torah scroll, stepped forward to meet him. But Nehemiah placed two fingers of his right hand against the purple covering of the scroll, next placed them against his lips and then approached the table of the judges. Bowing above this table he fixed his eyes upon the face of his brother.

Above the bowed youth the narrating judge said. "This waxen figure was found this morning by three publicans; they brought it here and placed it before the court. None knows where nor when nor why nor by whom the form and traits of your brother were given to this image."

"It is known to the Court on High where and when

this image assumed the form and the traits of my brother, in order to appear before this court and bear witness to that, to which it will bear witness in the presence of the Court on High." Thus Nehemiah made his reply to the narrating judge.

And Nehemiah lifted up that form from the table of the judges, even as one lifts up the Torah scroll after the reading of the portion is completed, and he turned his own face as well as the face of his brother Jochanan toward the Messenger and he said: "In the name of my brother Jochanan, slain as a desecration of the Name, and in the names of all the children of Israel, who were slain as a desecration and defilement of the Name, and in the name of those eleven hundred thousand, who went to their deaths for the Sanctification of the Name—in all their names I say: Creator of all Worlds, the measure of suffering for the sake of Thy Name is now full and overflowingly full.

"For two thousand years they have been shedding our blood on this continent. And the earth of this continent, other than the earth of an immemorial and purer time, does not open its mouth to cry to Heaven, when it has been defiled by blood. No, the earth of this continent opens its bloody jaws in order to drink the blood that overflows.

"Now worse things have come to pass than were ever foretold for the end of time. Wherever a rod of farming land gleams in the sun, there lie the murdered bones of our brothers. Wherever a river in its green banks curves gracefully about a hill, there once its waters were red with our blood. Wherever in wild nights of storm there is weeping, it is the weeping of our mothers, our sisters, our children. In the thousand nights of the sombre years, the while we dwelt in subterranean caverns, we heard that weeping and we say now: the measure of our suffering in exile is full and overflowing.

"With prayer and beseeching we would bring about the end of our exile. And if we cannot bring about this end by prayer and by beseeching, we will wrest it from

Heaven. We will break forth from this exile. We will go whither our eyes lead us. And these eyes of ours will lead us thither, where we have fixed them for two thousand years. Thrice on every day, when we assume the posture of our prayers, we turn our countenances toward the east and our eyes gaze forth toward Jerusalem. Thrice on every day we say: 'On account of our sins were we cast forth out of our own land and separated from our own earth.' But have our sins not been expiated? Were not the sufferings of a single generation in exile severe enough to atone for all our sins?

"On a plane which is higher than that of the prayer recalling the sins of our fathers, and higher than all the prayers which break out of the depth of our hearts, on that highest plane there shines a teaching which says: Israel was not driven out of its land; it was sent out into exile in order to carry forth the word of its scripture and the light of its teaching and to spread it abroad among the peoples of the earth.

"And on another level, as deep as the former one is high, there irradiates and frightens us at the same time another teaching, which declares: You are sent out into exile, in order to gather the sparks of holiness which fell into the impure abysses of darkness during the making of the world, when the vessels of Creation were broken. To gather up the lost sparks of Creation, over which the demons of the impure abysses came to rule, such is the mission of Israel in its exile.

"The light of the Torah in their hearts, girded with commandments, gifted with believing eyes, thus did they set out, our children, the searchers after those sparks. And they descended into those abysses, where the demons dwell, in order to gather in the lost sparks of Creation.

"Now have the demons torn out the believing eyes of our children and made of their hearts a clod of desecrated blood. With twice eleven hundred thousand torn-out children's eyes this truth stares also into your face, O Messenger. And the eyes ask: Are the lost sparks safe? Is

131

the work accomplished? Has the mission come to an end?"

At this Nehemiah had once more lifted high the form before him into the clear sight of the Messenger and now fell silent in expectation of the Messenger's answer. A heavy and sombre silence had descended upon the Hall of Prayer of the old synagogue, as though all light had suddenly fled from the sun of day. And as this darkness extended and no breath of an answer vibrated in the oppressive emptiness, the judges themselves took fright and encouraged their youthful proclaimer to further speech.

But a great weakness had overcome the youth Nehemiah. His arms were weary with the too-heavy weight of his brother's form, and his delicate figure swayed under the weight of that which bore the shape of his brother.

Now there arose in the old synagogue, a deep and tranquil voice, even as it had arisen on that most dreaded of all dread days. It was the voice of the man Michael, called Mechzio; audibly to all it said to Nehemiah: "Let not the Messenger depart unless he give you an answer. With that form in your arms you are stronger than he. Because he is one who merely stands. You are a wanderer and a bearer. Go to the Messenger and let him carry that form, of which the weight is as heavy as the weight of the whole world."

Nehemiah looked around after the *Ab Beth-Din*, who stood beside him with the rescued Torah scroll. At the sight of the Torah, Nehemiah took courage and once more his eyes were bright with confidence. Without seeking the approval of the *Ab Beth-Din*, he took the silver crown of the scroll, placed it, to the visible consternation of all the judges, upon the head of the form in his arms, and said:

"You messengers beside us and you messengers afar from us, step back before this majesty! Step back and clear a path—not for me, but for my brother Jochanan, who speaks through my voice. Clear a path for him, that he may carry our prayers, our prayers and our questions, before that Tribunal on High, of Whose answer the majesty of this figure has made us worthy.

"But if you would not clear a path for my brother, then will I approach you, O Messenger beside us, and I will say to you in my voice: Give us the answer! Reveal the message! Otherwise I will go to you and cast this form at your feet and declare: This is our last blood; this is our last prayer; this is our last word and this is our last summons. We have nothing beyond this."

And now it came to pass that the Messenger raised his voice and gave answer to Nehemiah with great gentleness, saying: "Nehemiah ben Zacharia Hakohen, you have said with your own voice that here and today you would pray for an answer, beseech it to be given you, demand it. Behold, with the voice of your brother, which in the days that he lived even your father could never distinguish from your voice, you have by prayer, by beseeching, by demand brought forth the answer.

"The answer is brief, because it brings a great message. The message consists of two words. The first word retains light from the light of Origin. The second word has light from the light of the End." And the Messenger raised his voice so high that it sounded like a resounding light and he set to an echoing the very air within the old synagogue. And the two words are: *Athhalta di-Geulah!*"

"*Athhalta di-Geulah,*" said Nehemiah, repeating the words of the Messenger softly, like one in a dream. And as he saw the Messenger disappear, he himself, holding high that form, sank to his knees. And even as the *Kohanim* on Yom Kippur, he fell upon his face and prayed: "Praised be the High Name of His rule in time and eternity." And he held the form next to him in brotherly fashion and repeated the prayer seven times.

The judges surrounded the *Ab Beth-Din* who had fallen into an ecstatic silence and who only now recovered the power of speech. Then all prayed and all spoke the blessing: "Praised beest Thou, O Lord, King of all Eternities, that Thou has preserved us in life and has let us last and endure unto this day."

Then two of the judges, the narrating judge and Reb Senderl, approached Nehemiah, who was holding high the form in his hands, and helped Nehemiah raise himself up again. And they carried that form to the table of the judges and wrapped it in a prayer shawl and left upon its head the crown of the Torah, which Nehemiah had placed there.

"Like that pillar of fire by night, like that pillar of cloud by day," said Nehemiah, "thus will this our third pillar, the pillar of blood lead us through all the wildernesses into the Holy Land. *Athhalta di-Geulah!* Redemption has begun! Next year in Jerusalem!"

The *Ab Beth-Din* gave the Torah scroll to the narrating judge. Then he put his arms around Nehemiah and kissed him and said: "The answer of the Messenger was *Athhalta di-Geulah.* That is to say: The beginning of redemption. Redemption is perfection, and perfection cannot set in suddenly. A great rabbi has taught us: Redemption will set in gradually as a transformation of all things. Redemption will not come like a storm wind with lightning and thunder. What is crooked will be made straight. Every thing which is falsely placed will altar its position a little and so be rightly placed. And that will be redemption.

"We, however, will not be permitted to be idle witnesses of the process of perfection, even as we were never permitted to be idle witnesses in the expectation of the Messiah. Even as we had to compel the beginning of redemption, so we will have to compel its fulfillment. And as a sign of the attainment of perfection will the Messiah appear. But creating here means achievement through suffering. And there is no vicarious suffering, even as there is no vicarious remorse and expiation.

"And as redemption was foretold, so also were foretold the sufferings, the *heblei leda*, the sufferings which precede the birth of redemption. We all know how great were the sufferings which have already been endured. How great will be the suffering still to come is known only to the Creator of the Universe, Who in His grace has renewed our hearts toward a new life. For the redemption has begun.

"And now let us thank the Creator and renew our prayers, even as He has renewed our hearts. Let us then pray and say: Creator of all Worlds, we would return to the pure springs of our earth and to the living fountains of Thy teaching. We would no longer warm ourselves at alien hearths nor taste of alien meats nor drink of impure springs.

"But you, Nehemiah ben Zacharia Hakohen, are in-

135

deed blessed. You have been found worthy of receiving the great answer of the Messenger. May your strength be increased. You have received the answer, because you asked in the name of the eleven hundred thousand children, who fell sacrificed to the Torah. For our children are our warranty.

"It came to pass in the great hour of Revelation, when our people stood at the foot of Sinai, prepared to receive the Torah. Then spoke the Creator of the World to it: 'I will give you the Torah. But can you give me warranties, that you will guard the Torah and fulfill it?' 'Yes!' cried the people. 'Let our three arch-fathers, Abraham, Isaac and Jacob, be our guarantors.' But the Creator of the World made answer: 'No, your arch-fathers did many things which were not pleasing unto Me. Provide Me with others.'

" 'The prophets may stand for us,' cried the people. 'Take, Lord, the word of our prophets as our warranty!' 'No,' said the Creator of the World. 'In their burning love of man and in the fire of their word, the prophets will make additions to the Law and also encourage their later followers and imitators to subtract from the Law. Provide Me with other guarantors!'

" 'Let our children stand for us,' cried the people. 'Let them be our warranty!' 'Your children,' said the Lord, 'yes, your children will suffice Me. For the sake of your children, will I give you the Torah.' You put your question well, Nehemiah, when you put it in the name of our children."

Nehemiah stood like one in a dream before the *Ab Beth-Din* and said: "Rabbi, you heard the words which I had the strength to speak with this, our pillar of blood, in my arms. But when suddenly a great fear and weakness came upon me, which made rigid my lips and caused me to be silent, my praying did not cease but continued in my heart and it spoke on in both thought and word.

"As on that bloody Yom Kippur in this synagogue, as again later in the many dreadful visions of the many

136

nights, I stood again yonder, on that place, where I saw the brains of the slain children dashed against the wall; even as on that day I saw once again the murderer, who slew my brother, and I remembered how, in my horror, I prayed to the Creator of the World to give me the strength, Oh, to give me the strength of this murderer, that I might instantly slay him, even as he had slain my brother—

"Even as on that day I saw the murderer, neck of steer, bristle of swine, eye of wolf, teeth of dog. And even as on that day something cried out within me: No, O Master of all Worlds, do not give me the strength of this murderer! Let me keep the believing eyes of my brother. Let me but have his eyes and his feebleness! And let me be a sacrifice among the other sacrifices and not a murderer among murderers.

"But otherwise than on that day, when I had but a premonition of the truth, it was now revealed to me in its entirety: he who feels this, thinks this, and only he who feels and thinks thus, is a child of Jaacob-Yisrael, of whatever name or race or faith he be. He who feels and thinks otherwise is a son of Cain-Esau, whatever be his name or race or faith.

"Creator of the World, we will renew our prayers even as Thou hast renewed our hearts. We know that a time will come when there will exist on earth no strong and no weak, no hunters and no hunted, no oppressors and no oppressed, no slayers and no slain, no masters and no servants, no rich and no poor.

"For we know that this world is no waiting room for eternity. Eternity is here among us. Therefore we are bidden not to take thought for our own thereafter, but for our brothers' welfare in this world. And we know that this teaching will survive all its enemies and all our own. Are our enemies more mighty than we? But our Torah is stronger than their might, and our dream is greater than their night.

"The evil time is at an end. For redemption has begun. But so long as evil still dwells in the world for the

137

peoples of the world and, above all, for Thy people, O Creator of Eternity, let us, while there still are oppressors and oppressed, be among the oppressed and not among the oppressors, among the hunted and not the hunters, among the slain and not the slayers.

"Above all, Creator of the Universe, let us continue to side with the humble and not with the arrogant. We know that this world will be saved from evil. Should this not be true, may we know nothing further; for nothing further will be worth knowing."

THE TWENTY-THIRD CHAPTER

In the meantime another group of Red soldiers had appeared at the entrance of the old synagogue. The soldiers came down the steps in two rows and, with mechanical precision and silent swiftness, as though it were a military parade, they formed a straight espalier for their general who entered with a Red Commissar beside him. By the side of the Commissar went that youngest among the publicans who, after every battle, had always been the first to offer himself as a spy to the conqueror.

"*Mi wsio znajem!*" cried the Commissar at once from the highest step. "We know everything!" he repeated and continued speaking, as he descended the steps by the side of the general. "We have fixed up this matter of redemption. We didn't need miracles. We have uprooted wealth; and, you see, when there's no wealth, there's no poverty either." And he was evidently ready to make a long speech. But in view of the frightened little group of people before them, the general waved him aside.

Although they knew that, in all probability, they need fear no immediate brutality from the intruders, yet the sudden entry of soldiers frightened the judges, for it reminded them of that other intrusion of troops into the synagogue. Followed by four judges the *Ab Beth-Din*

139

hastened down from the Almemor to salute the victors. The narrating judge and the accusing judge remained on the Almemor, the former with the Torah scroll, the latter with the pillar of blood upon the table.

And even as on that dreadful day the old Rav had bowed down before the officer of the S.S., so now did the *Ab Beth-Din* salute the Red general, filled with the fear of the pious man before the bearer of arms and with gratitude to the liberator of the city. The two priests also accompanied the judges and saluted the victors in evident anxiety.

The Red general, a tall and quite young man, received these salutations in friendly fashion and replied to the greeting of peace offered him by the *Ab Beth-Din* with a shake of the hand. Then both the general and the Commissar regarded the paintings on the wall. Next they expressed the wish to see the form on the Almemor, adding once more, with sympathy, the words: *"Mi wsio znajem."*

Obviously shocked by what they had seen, they descended from the Almemor. Then the general caught sight of the two German uniforms and asked sharply: "Why are these two still here? Why have these two murderers not been taken care of?" "They were left with the court until the close of the proceedings," the Commissar, who seemed really to be well informed, told him. "Now they will be taken out and the sentence will be executed."

The wounded soldier approached the general in military tread. He placed himself at attention in front of the general and said for all to hear: "I take the liberty of reporting myself as not having belonged to the S.S. formation. I was wounded this morning. The S.S. men found me in the ruins of a house and dragged me here. But I am not one of them; I am a soldier."

"Cowardly dog! Traitor!" the S.S. officer roared at him and, beside himself with rage, he plunged toward the publican Andrej. With the cry: "That is my pistol!" he tore the weapon from Andrej's hands and shot the soldier from behind through the wounded head. But he crashed to the floor with his victim, felled by a blow of the forest fighter Mechzio, who at once disarmed him and dragged him up again by the collar.

"Take him out to the square and have him hanged there with the other murderers," the general ordered his soldiers who had hastened down from the steps and secured the madman. The forest fighter Mechzio, however, went to the painted wall, took the empty box which stood in front of the smaller figure of the crucified one, pointed out the inscription to the general and said:

"General, this S.S. murderer is responsible for the bloody deeds in the municipal forest. He forced thousands of men and women and children to dig their own mass grave, before he had them shot down. This box bears the words: 'Property of the German Army.' Let this murderer, as the Messenger foretold, carry this box, which is German property, as his coffin on his way to the gallows."

At a gesture of the general the two soldiers released the S.S. officer who, until that moment, had preserved his insolent bearing in the extremity of arrogant self-deception. But when Mechzio showed him the box, which was to be his coffin, the terror of death overcame him and he trembled so violently that he was unable to hold the box.

This being so, Mechzio lifted up the box and pressed it down over the head of the condemned man. Two soldiers took his arms, pressed their shoulders against his and thus dragged him, groping blindly with his feet and dangling his legs like a jumping jack up the steps and out toward the gallows.

"We cannot bring back to life the victims of the German madness. But the criminals will not escape punishment. You are now under our protection. The German terror is over," said the Red Commissar.

It was now Nehemiah who addressed the Commissar. His voice was clear and strong: "What happens here concerns us no longer. We would stay here no more. This

141

morning, after five years in the graves and caves, we saw the town for the first time again by the light of day. It is a broken shard. But we saw that the market place has been repaved. And for the new pavement they used the grave-stones from our cemetery. They did not even take care to reverse the stones, so as to hide the letters that spell the names of our dead. We will not stay here. We will take the rescued Torah scroll; we will take that form from the judge's table and we will set forth and wander onward until we reach the Holy Land, the Land of Israel, our land. Next year in Jerusalem."

"Jerusalem, your Jerusalem, has been a heap of ruins for two thousand years," jeered the Commissar. "Your land, the Land of Israel, holy or not, what good is it for millions and millions? There isn't any more rain of manna and of roast quail in the desert, you know."

"Our Jerusalem was never a city of stone," said the narrating judge. "Our Jerusalem was light; the light of the heart, the heart of the world for all mankind. It is true that our land is a small land. But one third of our people have fallen in the holocaust of this continent. We, whom they have left behind to mourn them, we would not re-main here. For us the book of this continent is closed. It is not for us to add even an epilogue."

"We are beginning a new book of history," said the Commissar, "which will be the book not only of this conti-nent. You are free, like every other people, to write your chapter in this book, if you will cooperate with us. If you do not, the wheel of history will crush you as it rolls over you."

Thereupon the *Ab Beth-Din* raised his voice and spoke to the Commissar: "Many wheels of history have rolled over us into the abysses of the night and plunged with broken axles into the darkness of oblivion, the while we have ever arisen again, we, who are the perpetual wit-nesses of the Creator, we, who are the companions of Eter-nity. Even if you speak the truth, we would write no more

142

chapters in alien books. Whatever our brothers in other continents decide to do—we, the remnant of those who once were, we are going home. 'For I will establish them in their land, that they be no more cast forth from their land, which I have given them, saith the Lord.' "

THE TWENTY-FOURTH CHAPTER

At this point the Red Commissar explained to the judges as well as to the priests that he would send out a group of skilled artisans in order to cleanse the painted wall from those images of shame and mockery. Then he followed his general who was waiting impatiently on the steps.

But now it came to pass that the wife of the Torah scribe, leaning upon the girl Esther, placed herself in the path of the Red Commissar. She seized the sleeve of his coat and said to him: "You have told us a story about a redemption that has long begun in your country. This Messenger of ours, very generous with his prophecies, has just proclaimed the beginning of redemption too. But just a few hours before the beginning of our redemption, they murdered my husband down there, in the clay caverns. Do you know that, Commissar?

"My husband was the Torah scribe of this city. He was a good man and a pious man. All the days of his life he did harm to none. Look, there he lies upon the earth and his son, our son, cannot say *Kaddish* for his father, because there are not ten men left to form a *minyan*.

"There were twenty-six thousand of our faith in this town and of these not ten men are left alive to constitute a *minyan*. That is the price paid for our redemption. I do not ask whether the price was not too great. Perhaps that would be a sin. But perhaps it would be no sin if I ask you, Commissar: How great was the price of redemption in your country? Are there any left there fit to complete a *minyan*? Is there among your soldiers a tenth man fit for a *minyan*, so that we can say *Kaddish* for a Torah scribe?"

"Are there not even ten men left of twenty-six thousand in this accursed town?" cried the Commissar. He turned a questioning glance at the two priests and seemed particularly surprised at the circumstance that he had not, in fact, known everything. "Was the publican Andrej the only human being who stood on the side of the victims? What did you two shepherds do to prevent your flocks from howling and biting and rending with the wolves?"

"We were powerless," said the younger priest, "and we had no orders from our superiors to intervene." With a glance at the general, who was now no longer impatient, the Commissar said: "The German murderers declare themselves innocent, because they merely followed the command of their superiors. And these declare themselves innocent, because they had received no command from *their* superiors. What a world!

"It is not my office to chide priests. I know nothing of such things. But when I was a child I read something in *their* Scripture concerning the story of Cain and Abel. Did not Cain give that same reply when he was asked: 'Cain, where is thy brother Abel?' "

Although the Commissar had meant this question to be a purely rhetorical one, yet he paused for a few moments, as though expecting an answer. Then he bent down to the tiny shriveled wife of the Torah scribe and, making his voice appropriately small, he said to her: "Grandmother, there will hardly be found even a single one among my soldiers who still shares your superstition concerning *minyan* and *Kaddish*."

Suddenly the voice of the publican Andrej was heard. He had stepped aside, discouraged and ashamed

145

that he had let the S.S. officer snatch the pistol from him. He said: "I could swear that there is still one other hidden here. He is none of those whom I guarded; he has been here for a few months only. Once, by night, I caught sight of his shadow. But he disappeared and there was no trace of him, as though the very wall had devoured him. How he survived the final week is hard to tell, because for a whole week I did not dare to provide either food or water."

"Perhaps it is one of the thousands who were murdered," said the Commissar. "Perhaps a man will arise from the dead here. So many signs and wonders have taken place, that the miracle of all miracles might be revealed here, namely, a resurrection from the dead." With sharp finger the Commissar pointed to the larger image of the crucified on the wall. "That one is said to have arisen. Why should He not step down from the image of Him there?" Thus speaking, the Commissar drew his pistol from his holster. "To express their scorn both of us and of Him, they have placed a Red Star where His heart would be and so He has calmly witnessed all these horrors. Was He not a Jew, too? Would it not be the right and proper thing if He were now to step down from the wall and be that sorely needed tenth man for the *Kaddish* prayer?" And therewith the Commissar stretched out his arm, and, taking careful aim, fired with precision at the figure of the crucified and transpierced the red star which was its heart.

A fragment splintered from the stone on which the red star had been painted. As though the bullet had hit a secret spring, which set a mechanism in motion, a narrow door, let into the wall, which had been painted over with the figure of the crucified one, opened slowly and silently. In the dimness of the framework of this suddenly revealed door there stood, like a statue in a niche, a pallid, black-bearded man in tattered garments. They were stained with clay and with traces of blood and pus about the chest and arms. The man scarce held himself erect on tottering legs. With elbows lifted sidewise and leaning against the masonry, he gave the appearance of hanging lifelessly in that

146

niche. His face was shriveled; scabbed scratches marked it; his closed eyes were white as those of one dead.

In the face of this half-dead man in the niche the younger priest fell into a great excitement. Perhaps the suddenly fired shot had frightened him; perhaps he had not seen the door in the wall open. He folded his hands and said with quivering voice: *"Domine, non sum dignus . . ."* But the fat priest took him by the arm and kept him from kneeling down and calmed him: "That is, in all likelihood, the Jew whom the publican was talking about and saying that he had been hidden here for weeks."

"Why, that is our Avreml, the basso, who used to sing in our choir here," cried Reb Senderl. "Of all people, they want to talk Latin with Avreml, the basso!" His voice was plaintive now. He hurried up to the wall and lifted the man out of that niche as easily as though he had been a child. "Water—water," the famished man whispered and opened his eyes. But they could not bear the light of day and closed again at once.

Andrej fetched a field flask from one of the Red soldiers and Reb Senderl let the famished man drink. "Don't be afraid, Avreml, Amalek has been beaten. Drink slowly, just one little swallow," said Reb Senderl to the trembling man whom he held upright with his right arm while, with the left, he put the flask against his swollen lips.

The famished man took a greedy swallow and lifted up his hands in order to secure the flask. His arms were as thin as those of a ten-year old child and his fingers had not the strength to hold the bottle. "More water—more— more," he whispered when Reb Senderl drew the flask away a little. "I was in the death camp in Janov—torture —torture—in Maidanek—in Treblinka—torture—torture —everywhere—" the man whispered so feebly, that only Reb Senderl could understand him. "I worked in a quarry —more water—a little water—something crashed—the stones covered me—they thought I was dead—I was hidden—I ran away by night—water—water—"

Reb Senderl eased him down carefully on the floor

147

and gave him more water. The man moved his lips: "I ran from forest to forest—from field to field. I slept by day in the forests—I ran by night across the fields—home—across the fields toward home—my father once showed me the door in the wall—I ran and ran to the door in the wall—they would not find me there. For a while a good man brought bread and water by night. Then there was no bread—no water. Then I forgot how to open the door. No strength—to open the door—the door—the door—" And once more Avreml, the basso, opened his sightless eyes and with these eyes still open fell backwards and was dead.

There was silence for a space. Then the wife of the Torah scribe lifted up her voice and wept. And the general said to the Commissar: "You're a fine marksman, you are. You almost produced a miracle! That would have been fine for you—to have to report a miracle to Moscow. That will teach you not to shoot in old synagogues."

At the same time the youngest of the publicans whispered to Andrej: "You see, I always told you that another Jew was hidden here who painted the pictures and paints them back again by night. These Jews can do anything!"

But since the wife of the Torah scribe continued her disconsolate wailing, the general turned to his soldiers and said to them: "If there is one among you who is fit to be the tenth man for this praying, let him step forward." The soldiers, standing in their two rows, examined each other silently, as though the general had asked for volunteers upon a most dangerous mission. To the amazement of the general not a single volunteer made himself known. "We have six hundred thousand Jewish soldiers in our army. Isn't there a single one here?"

Suddenly at this moment the publican Andrej stretched out a trembling hand toward the wall, where the pictures were and cried out thrice in a throttled voice. All eyes turned to the wall. The wailing of the old woman ceased. And even as a swarm of frightened birds suddenly soars high in the air, thus rustled forth from that company

148

a sight of speechless wonder. For the pictures that had been upon the wall, were there no more.

The judges surrounded Nehemiah and the partisan Mechzio and held each other by the arms and swayed in unison as in an unstirring dance. And the *Ab Beth-Din* pronounced the blessing that is to be pronounced over a wondrous event and all the others repeated the blessing after him, word for word.

"A miracle, a true miracle," the publican Andrej cried out in a loud voice. "Think of all the things the Jews can do!" said the youngest publican and followed on the heels of Andrej, who was running to the priests, in order to get expert confirmation from their lips.

The fat priest said: "We will inform our superiors concerning this miracle." The younger priest said: "I will report to my bishop exactly what my eyes have seen. My bishop will institute a careful investigation as to what has happened here and report to Rome. Then Rome will decide whether it was a miracle."

Simultaneously an almost similar colloquy took place between the general and the Commissar. The general said: "You'll have to report a miracle to Moscow after all, Comrade." "Why should I?" the Commissar objected. "You're the commander here, Comrade." "No," said the general. "Miracles are none of my business. Miracles belong to the department of religion and, from our point of view, religion belongs to the department of politics. And you're the political Commissar. So you will report. That is an order, Comrade." "All right," said the Commissar. "I will report everything to Moscow and Moscow will decide whether a miracle has taken place." "That is right," said the general. "And now I will do something, concerning which I will myself report to Moscow." Therewith the general took off his bandolier and gave it to the Commissar to hold. Then he pushed his fur cap deeper over his forehead and with a determined tread approached the judges. He spoke to the *Ab Beth-Din:*

"Rabbi, I am the son of a Jewish father and of a Jew-

149

ish mother. I cannot pray and I do not believe in God. But if, according to your laws, I am fit to be the tenth needed for your praying—very well! War is war. Miracles might come in handy even in the army."

With both hands the *Ab Beth-Din* took the hand of the general and greeted him with the salutation of peace: "According to our Law you are still one of us. You say you have no faith? Yet you did fight against Amalek. In this place and in this hour you did smite Amalek. And so we bless you. May you be here the first, not the tenth, in our *minyan*."

The other members of the *minyan* now greeted the general with the salutation of peace. While this took place two other soldiers stepped out of line and hastened down the steps and stood at attention, offering to join in the prayer. The general nodded at them with a nod of understanding and said to the *Ab Beth-Din:* "Rabbi, get it over quickly. We didn't march to the Seret in order to pray. Amalek, as you call him, is in flight and he runs quickly."

The *Ab Beth-Din* turned to Nehemiah and said to him: "Your father, Zacharia Hakohen, died on this day for the Sanctification of the Name. Be you our precentor." The men turned their faces toward the east and Nehemiah said the *Kaddish*. He used the plain and simple chant that is used for the *Kaddish* on weekdays. But his prayer sounded like the *Kaddish* chant which is used as the Day of Dread comes to an end: all the great chants have been chanted and all the heaven-storming prayers have declined and all tears have been shed and all the fervor of the heart has burned itself out. And then, suddenly, the little light of common day appears again—the great *Kaddish* in its simple vesture, and in the melody of the ordinary days of the week.

But it is a melody as deeply aware as the spirit itself, as articulate as speech itself, and it says rather than sings: I know how difficult, how dangerous, how piteous it is to be a human being. I know, too, how fair and great and glorious it is to be a human being. Therefore, whenever ten are assembled I say: Yes—to the greatness of the Creator. I say Yes—to the holiness of the Creator. I say Yes—to the eternity of the Creator. Thrice on each day do I say: Yes—to the greatness, to the holiness, the eternity of the Creator, and of the Creation and of all creatures:

YISGADAL V'YISKADASH SHEMEI RABBA